"I'm not interested in your kind of game."

"I don't have a game in mind," Alex replied with a touch of whimsy. "More like a contract. I don't think you could classify a marriage contract as a game."

Kate searched his expression for any trace of mockery. "What's that supposed to mean?" she asked.

His eyes were watchful, even though his manner appeared relaxed. His hand moved in an airy gesture of invitation. "Tell me what you want for the rest of your life."

"Working on the principle that money buys everything," she mocked.

"Not at all. It buys comfort and freedom. It doesn't buy children."

She knew as he spoke those last words that he had perceived her own dearest wish and was using it, calmly, knowingly, and to devastating effect.

Books by Emma Darcy

HARLEQUIN PRESENTS
648—TWISTING SHADOWS
680—TANGLE OF TORMENT
823—DON'T PLAY GAMES

These books may be available at your local bookseller.

Don't miss any of our special offers. Write to us at the following address for information on our newest releases.

Harlequin Reader Service
P.O. Box 52040, Phoenix, AZ   85072-2040
Canadian address: P.O. Box 2800, Postal Station A,
5170 Yonge St., Willowdale, Ont.   M2N 6J3

EMMA DARCY

don't play games

Harlequin Books

TORONTO • NEW YORK • LONDON
AMSTERDAM • PARIS • SYDNEY • HAMBURG
STOCKHOLM • ATHENS • TOKYO • MILAN

Harlequin Presents first edition October 1985
ISBN 0-373-10823-0

Original hardcover edition published in 1985
by Mills & Boon Limited

CHAPTER ONE

'HURRY up, damn you!'

The silent curse grew louder in her mind as Kate watched her husband pour out a few more honeyed compliments and exchange a couple of witticisms. Once again he had taken too long to seat their guests around the table. The soup had already been ladled out. She seethed with impatience as he delayed its serving. Scott was overplaying his role of genial host. He was on a super-ego trip tonight, all because Alex Dalton had come to dinner.

Kate's eyes fixed dubiously on the big man who had just taken the chair next to her place at the table. A man as wealthy as Alex Dalton would not be impressed. This dinner-party was a waste of time and effort . . . and money. She had seen the cynicism in his eyes as pre-dinner drinks and hors d'oeuvres had been served. His manner had been affable enough but those eyes had carried a different message. Alex Dalton was not going to be wined and dined into a business deal.

At last everyone was settled. Kate swiftly produced the first course and slid into her chair at the end of the table, forestalling Alex Dalton's move to help her. 'Please start,' she murmured with an anxious flutter in her heart. She had spent hours making this wretched beetroot soup because the man Scott wanted to impress had expressed a liking for borscht.

'The soup is cold,' Scott said slowly and emphatically.

Kate winced and tasted. It was barely warm. 'Sorry, darling,' she muttered, the soft words covering a fierce desire to tip the contents of his soup-plate all over him. She imagined the stunned horror on his face as the beetroot-red stain soaked into his Dior shirt, the Cardin silk tie and the elegantly tailored suit. A small, secret smile tilted the corners of her mouth.

'I prefer borscht at this temperature. The flavour is more pronounced. It's the best I've tasted for a long time.' The tone was authoritative and the delivery so deliberate that the words could only be taken as a challenge to Scott's criticism.

'You're very kind, Mr Dalton. Thank you,' Kate added politely, although she did not feel grateful. Her only feeling towards Alex Dalton was resentment.

Sharp blue eyes noted her reserve and a spark of amusement glinted briefly. 'My name is Alex, and few people would call me kind.'

Scott gave one of his short, sophisticated laughs. 'I'm not surprised. You're a hard man to do business with.'

'I never suffer fools gladly,' was the bland reply.

Scott cocked one eyebrow, all too sure of himself. 'I don't imagine you do. But a smart man who knows what goods to deliver is worth your time.'

'It takes a very smart man to know that,' Alex Dalton agreed with a slight curl to his lips. The blue eyes swept back to Kate, coolly appraising. 'The only question is, how good are the goods?'

'That's surely for you to decide,' Kate said evenly, not wanting to be drawn into a business discussion. That was Scott's field, not hers.

'I shall need a little time to do that,' he replied sardonically.

Kate returned her attention to the soup. Alex Dalton could look elsewhere for conversation. The whole five years of her marriage seemed to have been spent currying favour with such men, men who had the power or the wealth or the influence which might get Scott what he wanted. Their life was a charade, one step ahead of bankruptcy. Hire-purchase and heavy interest payments on loans provided the façade of wealth. All their income was used to impress others and Kate hated the falseness of it all.

Sometimes she hated Scott too; hated him for his distorted sense of values, hated him for denying her children, hated him for deceiving her as to his real self. She regretted her marriage to him but the shared years still held her in bondage. She did not have the will to break free. A weak thread of optimism kept whispering that maybe one day he would change and see the error of his ways. Every day made that seem more improbable.

She watched him as he sipped the soup, observed his practised charm as he directed conversation around the table. He was handsome. There was no hint of weakness in his clean-cut features. The dark wavy hair was fashionably styled. Everything about Scott was fashionable. Even his physique had a polished cut, tall, muscular, athletic.

He was fashionably unfaithful too. She noted

Fiona Chardway flirting with him and the gleam of answering promise in Scott's hazel eyes. She wondered if Fiona was already sharing her bed with him. With a little jolt of shock Kate realised that such a thought no longer had the power to hurt her.

'Is Kate short for Catherine?'

She turned to Alex Dalton, surprised at the question and conscious that her silence had been too long. 'No. Kathleen.' A whimsical smile curved her mouth. 'Mary Kathleen, if the truth be told. Irish to the core, Mr Dalton. My maiden name was O'Malley.'

He nodded, his eyes drifting to the brilliant red-gold of her hair before returning to eyes more blue than his own. 'The colouring fits.' His slow grin expressed a very dry amusement. 'But the traditional temper is well in control. Would I be trying it too far if I asked for a second helping of borscht?'

'I'm afraid what's left in the tureen will certainly be cold,' she answered wryly.

'No matter. I'll enjoy it anyway.'

'If you insist.'

She removed his plate along with her own and carried them out to the kitchen. Having served him with the requested second helping, she deftly loaded the remaining empty plates on a tray, clearing the table in readiness for the next course. It was time to put the prepared vegetables on to cook. The fillets of beef were already in the oven and she prayed that tonight the Bearnaise sauce would not curdle. One mistake per dinner party was quite enough. Despite Alex Dalton's comment that her temper was in control, it felt very brittle.

She checked that everything was timed correctly and then returned to the dining-room. Scott was refilling glasses, burbling on about the merits of the red wine he was serving. So he should, Kate thought venomously. A '71 Grange at fifty dollars a bottle, was hardly a quaffing wine. Everyone seemed happy and convivial and Kate relaxed.

'Do you work, Mary Kathleen?'

The thought flitted through Kate's mind, 'You're drinking two days' work right now and I bet it doesn't mean a thing to you.' She forced a smile and answered lightly. 'Yes, I do some part-time secretarial work. I quite enjoy it and it takes me out of the house.'

'But you're not a career-woman.'

'No. I can't say I'm passionately attached to a typewriter.'

'So where do your passions lie?'

The question was put in a low, provocative tone. Kate sighed. A flirtation was the last thing she wanted. Her reply was deliberately off-putting. 'Probably in cooking.' After all, she had certainly felt heated over the cold soup.

'Why don't you have children?'

Why indeed? Kate gritted her teeth. She wanted to snap at him that she didn't have children because Scott wanted to be a big man like him. 'Do you have children, Mr Dalton?' she asked.

'No. I've never been married.'

It seemed odd that a man in his position had never taken a wife. Curiosity prompted her to take a more direct look at him. He was a big, powerfully built man, carrying more weight than he should. Despite his wealth he apparently disdained the extravagant flair of fashion. The dark grey lounge-suit was conventionally tailored and there was nothing remarkable about the plain white shirt. Even his tie was sober, tasteful but certainly not making a statement.

Kate suspected that to Alex Dalton clothes were simply a necessary adjunct to mixing in society. They had to be worn but all that was required of them was to suit the occasion. The mantle of success dressed him more forcefully than fashion and the man himself was statement enough. His presence would command attention in any company and honesty forced Kate to admit that it was this very essence which fed her resentment of his presence tonight.

Alex Dalton was not to blame for Scott's shortcomings but somehow his substance underlined her husband's superficiality. Scott posed. Alex Dalton was himself and had no need to be anyone else. Even his face was strong, his features blunt and uncompromising. The straight black hair was liberally streaked with grey and cut in a short, neat style. The slight upward kink at the end of his eyebrows gave his expression a sardonic air and the keen blue eyes held too much knowledge. They were glinting in amusement at her cold appraisal.

'You took your time.'

'I beg your pardon?' Kate flushed, taken aback by the light reprimand.

'Noticing me. Your aloofness was making me wonder. You play it very cool, Mary Kathleen, but I assume that iced water does not run through your veins.'

'I'm sorry if I've appeared preoccupied, Mr Dalton.'

'Alex.'

'I hope I haven't given offence.'

'Not at all. I am amused.'

'Amused?'

'Oh, I'm amused by all sorts of things. Do you like playing games, Mary Kathleen?'

'I'm not much good at games. Scott's the athlete.'

'In bed or out of it?'

He met her startled look with a keen watchfulness which made her shrink inside. 'Do you play golf, Mr Dalton?' she asked coolly.

His eyes mocked her sidestep. 'No. I prefer mental exercise, and you're succeeding in exercising my mind considerably. Why don't we follow an easier script?'

Kate frowned, not sure what he was implying. 'Is there a script to follow?' she replied cautiously.

'My dear, there's always a script where money is involved,' he said with soft derision. 'We both know that. The only question is in how the game is played.'

Kate could not repress the antagonism which flashed into her eyes. 'I think the pursuit of money brings more grief than happiness. Will you excuse me please? I must see to dinner.'

The brass of the man to expect her to suck up to him, Kate thought furiously. If he thought she was in the same mould as Scott he had another think coming.

The Bearnaise sauce curdled. Cursing her lack of concentration she dashed to the refrigerator for

some iced water. She poured it in drop by drop,
whisking furiously. Tears of frustration burnt her
eyes as the mixture remained separated. In
desperation she reached for a lemon, sliced it
through, squeezed a little juice and prayed. The
sauce was rescued. Almost sick with relief she
poured it into a sauce-boat and set it aside.

With smooth efficiency she removed the meat
from the oven, placed it on a carving tray, then
arranged the vegetables in serving dishes.
Assuming a calm, unhurried air she carried in the
meat-tray and placed it in front of Scott, following
up with the warmed dinner-plates as Scott
brandished the carving knife with his usual
expertise. By the time everything was laid out on
the table, Kate felt her inner tension easing. It all
looked steaming hot and appetising.

'The meat's a trifle overdone, Kate,' Scott
remarked critically.

'Tough!' she muttered under her breath.

'I hope not.'

She darted a startled glance at Alex Dalton.

He smiled. 'It looks perfect, pink and tender.
And the aroma of Bearnaise sauce is enough to
make any mouth water.'

'It curdled,' she said bluntly, not wanting his
praise.

'Did you look sourly at it?'

It was so true that she laughed, a pure ripple of
amusement which slowly degenerated into a
hiccup. She took a sip of wine and gave Alex
Dalton a dry look. 'A sour lemon rescued it.'

'Then praise be to lemons.' He gave both their
plates a generous dollop of sauce and then served
her as well as himself with vegetables.

'You obviously enjoy your food,' Kate remarked.

He raised one eyebrow suggestively. 'Among other things.'

'Why aren't you married?'

'Do you recommend it?'

She instantly sobered and retreated. 'You probably haven't felt the need.'

'Oh yes, I've felt the need.' There was almost a savage note of mockery in his voice. He seemed to pull himself back from whatever blackness was in his soul and continued with light flippancy. 'Maybe I've been too busy making that despised money, which does bring material comfort, if not happiness, or maybe I haven't found a woman I care to marry, or maybe I'm just too damned difficult to please. Take your pick.'

'Or maybe it suits you not to be tied down,' she retorted carelessly.

'Is the tie chafing you?'

Kate turned her attention to the meal in front of her. It was too personal a question for her to answer glibly and she had no intention of revealing how disillusioned she was with her marriage.

'Perhaps it helps to break loose occasionally. But then your husband doesn't keep a tight rein, does he?'

The provocative tone and the suggestion in the words made her bridle. 'You should be careful about making assumptions, Mr Dalton,' she said tightly.

A flash of irritation crossed his face. 'Fencing with formality can be overplayed. The name is Alex.'

'Surely such a successful man commands respect,' she mocked sweetly.

'We meet as social equals.'

'Was that in your script, Mr Dalton? Earlier this evening you implied that my role was that of a supplicant, softening you up for the kill.'

His eyes narrowed speculatively. Kate knew her tongue was running away from her but suddenly she felt reckless, uncaring of what this man thought. She reached for her wine-glass. It was empty. As usual Scott was so busy looking after his all-important guests that he had neglected her needs.

'Scott, would you pass the decanter down? Your wife has no wine,' Alex Dalton observed on a subtly critical note.

Scott's eyebrows shot up. 'Darling! How very remiss of me.' He immediately rose from his seat, carrying the decanter with him to make an elaborate show of looking after her. He topped up Alex Dalton's wine, thanked him for the timely reminder and proceeded to fill everyone's glasses, laughingly ignoring anyone's refusal. Scott prided himself on lavish hospitality. Most of it was paid for out of Kate's wage. She sipped the wine, wishing the dinner party was over and done with.

'So, you like to make your own terms.'

She looked blankly at Alex Dalton until she recalled her crack about a supplicant role. 'Doesn't everyone?' she asked carelessly.

'It depends if you're dealing from strength . . . and you do have strength,' he added with a wry smile. 'How old are you?'

'Do you always ply people with personal

questions? Don't you know a woman doesn't care to be asked her age?'

'Age doesn't worry you. At a guess I'd say twenty-five.'

'Seven. Two off. Almost three in fact. Birthdays keep rolling around,' she said on a note of despondency. She had very little to show for twenty-eight years.

'How long have you been married?'

'Five years.' Five, long, empty years, she added privately.

'Don't you want children?'

All her inner frustration flashed out at him for a moment. Then a cold mask settled on her face. 'That would be an extremely offensive question if I happened to be barren. As it happens, some people prefer to keep their lives uncomplicated by children. You're obviously one of them or you'd be married.'

'You're married,' he retorted pointedly.

'Yes, I'm married.' She looked down the table at her husband. He was titillating Fiona Chardway with a slightly risqué story. Kate had heard him tell it before. He did it well, holding the right pause before the punchline. Fiona laughed, patting his arm in appreciation and letting her hand linger there caressingly. That's my husband, Kate thought bitterly.

She glanced at Bob Chardway to see if he had noticed but he was deep in conversation with Jan Lister and Terry Jessell. Terry should be talking to Alex Dalton, she thought resentfully. He was Scott's business partner. Dennis Lister was clearly boring Wendy Jessell out of her mind. Kate wished someone would take Alex Dalton's attention away from her. She was not in the mood for his brand of chat.

Scott glanced up and caught her eye. He inclined his head slightly towards the kitchen. It was time to clear the table. Everyone had finished the meal. She quickly excused herself and went to work. She did not mind working and she could be by herself in the kitchen.

She took her time, checking that the oven temperature was just right before committing the orange soufflé to its mercy. She arranged some perfect strawberries on the cheese platter and stacked the dinner plates out of the way. Her mind drifted back over the short conversation with Alex Dalton.

Even if Scott would agree to having a baby Kate doubted that she wanted to bring a child into their marriage now. She did not want Scott's child. She wondered when her love had died and could not pinpoint the day or even the month. It had been slowly squeezed to death by his lies, his infidelities, his arrogant brushing aside of her needs as unimportant. The dull passivity she had fallen into was like a death. One day soon she would have to step out and meet life again before it was too late, before she became a complete robot.

She returned to the table with the cheeses. Everyone was enthusiastically discussing a yacht cruise on Sydney Harbour. She sat in silence, listening to the suggestions being thrown around, noticing that all the guests were deferring to Alex Dalton. From Scott's glowing accounts Kate assumed he was more than wealthy enough to own a yacht.

'You'll come of course,' he invited smoothly as he caught her eye.

'My skin doesn't like being out in the sun,' she remarked, preparing to excuse herself. The cruise would undoubtedly degenerate into an alcoholic binge and she did not care to watch Scott at play in that kind of scene.

'Part of the sundeck is shaded. I'll look after you,' he assured her.

Before she could reply Scott jumped in, answering for her, his eyes darting speculatively between Alex Dalton and herself. 'Kate loves being in the water. She'll be there, Alex.'

Kate froze. Her eyes were blue chips of ice, challenging Scott down the length of the table. Like hell I will, she projected to him and recognised the quick flare of temper which he suppressed. There would be a battle royal tonight but be damned if she would play his game. The business with Alex Dalton could hang on Scott's persuasion and whatever business acumen he possessed, not on her supposed charms.

'Then that's settled,' Alex Dalton said with an air of satisfaction.

Kate did not argue. Now was not the time for arguing.

'It must have been difficult for you as a child with your skin,' Alex Dalton suddenly commented.

'Yes. I was always made to cover up. I rebelled once. It was a lesson I never forgot. Second degree burns.'

His gaze fell to her bare shoulders. The white halter-necked dress she was wearing left her shoulders and back exposed to his view.

'There are no scars that I can see.'

'They faded. My fair skin has been a curse all my life. I couldn't go to the beach or really enjoy most outdoor activities.'

'I daresay that improved your skill at indoor activities,' he said with a twist of irony. 'I wouldn't say it was a curse. Your skin gleams like beautiful porcelain ... or better. I've had to repress the urge to touch it all night.'

She laughed a little wildly. 'I'm glad you repressed it. I'm not a china doll, Mr Dalton, nor do I like playing touching games,' she added, her tone void of all amusement.

He looked at her speculatively for a moment. Then with a slight curl of the lips he said, 'That's quite an extraordinary statement. Please enlighten me on what games you do like playing. You have me intrigued.'

'I like a straightforward play. Why don't you try it sometime?' she almost snapped at him, impatient with his innuendoes.

'Oh, I shall. I certainly shall, in my own good time and chosen place,' he answered derisively.

It was time to check the soufflé and Kate was glad of the excuse to escape from the uncomfortable conversation.

The soufflé had risen like a dream. Feeling pleased with herself Kate carried it into the dining-room. Everyone made delighted comments as it was served and tasted. Even Scott complimented her.

'A woman who cooks like this is a pearl beyond price,' Alex Dalton remarked.

'Kate took a Cordon Bleu course just after we

were married,' Scott informed him. 'She loves cooking, don't you, darling?'

'Yes,' she answered briefly.

'I'm afraid my talents lie elsewhere,' Fiona sighed.

Kate's lips thinned. I bet, she thought grimly.

The other two women discussed their favourite recipes, the men joining in with criticism or praise. Kate ate her soufflé, enjoying every mouthful as the tangy orange flavour melted on her tongue. There was only the coffee to be served now. She hoped the guests would not linger and make it a late night. The conversation drifted on to restaurants, opinions varying as to the merits of their cuisine. Alex Dalton aired a well-travelled knowledge and she tried to remember what Scott had told her about him.

The roots of his business empire lay in fruit-juice and cordials. Apparently he now held an interest in a fast-food company which had begun promoting its wares in Australia. Scott was trying to interest him in a new microwave device which freshened and crisped bread rolls. It was another one of Scott's high-flying schemes, playing agent to an inventor who had yet to produce a commercial proposition. It seemed almost eccentric of Alex Dalton to have accepted this dinner invitation.

'You look so pensive. What are you thinking?' he quietly asked.

Surprised by the soft query she answered bluntly. 'I was wondering why you're here.'

Surprise flickered in his eyes for a moment and then was gone, replaced by a weary cynicism. 'You know why I'm here. I accepted your husband's invitation.'

Kate shrugged. 'You could have chosen not to.'

He smiled and there was something uncomfortably suggestive in its curve. 'But I didn't choose not to. Call it a whim if you like.'

'Is the cruise also a whim?'

For a moment he paused. His gaze flicked to Scott and a ruthless gleam hardened his eyes. 'No, not a whim. I'm reciprocating your husband's so very kind hospitality.'

'I see,' she murmured, thinking that Scott would need to be on his toes tomorrow.

'I doubt it, Mary Kathleen,' he replied softly.

She threw him a puzzled look but was only answered by a sardonic smile which played about his lips. It made Kate notice their attractive sensuality.

'But I'm sure we'll understand each other tomorrow.'

The tone was low, intimate. She frowned and replied stiffly, 'I doubt that, Mr Dalton. It would be a waste of time for both of us.' She directed her gaze to the head of the table. 'Scott, shall I serve the coffee here?'

'No, thank you, darling. We'll move to the lounge.'

He rose and held out Fiona's chair for her. It was the signal for a general exodus and Kate withdrew once more into the kitchen. When she wheeled the trolley into the lounge she was kept busy pouring out coffee and offering after-dinner mints. Scott was dispensing liqueurs from the bar but most of the guests settled for coffee.

It was Alex Dalton who made the first move to leave. He remained firm in his intention despite

Scott's urging him to have more coffee, a brandy, a liqueur, anything at all which confirmed Scott's quality as a host. Kate silently accompanied their V.I.P. guest to the door. She wished him gone, wished them all gone. He turned and surprised her by taking her hand. The blue eyes demanded her attention and only hers. He completely ignored Scott.

'Thank you. I look forward to the pleasure of meeting you again.' The words carried a suggestion of intimacy.

Kate bridled. She almost snatched her hand away and would have stepped back, away from his closeness, but at that moment Scott put his arm around her in a possessive hug.

'Didn't I tell you I had a marvellous wife?' he said smugly.

Kate gritted her teeth at his hypocrisy. Scott was all show, all glib talk. In another moment he would be hurrying back to Fiona Chardway and his 'marvellous wife' might as well not exist.

There was a derisive gleam in Alex Dalton's eyes as he answered softly, 'Yes, you have a marvellous wife. 'Till tomorrow then, Scott.'

'Great!'

Kate winced at her husband's excessive enthusiasm. Alex Dalton threw an oddly questioning look at her, then departed, moving briskly.

Scott turned to her with a triumphant grin. 'How about that? Invited to a cruise, no less!'

She returned a sour smile. 'I think it's rather more than that. I'm not sure what he's about but I'd watch my step tomorrow if I were you.'

The cocksureness in his expression took a

cynical turn. 'He fancies you.' It was almost as if it diminished Alex Dalton in his eyes.

Kate lifted her chin and looked her scorn at him. 'You're a fool, Scott. The show's over for tonight. I'm going to bed.'

'Don't take that tone with me, Kate,' he warned nastily.

She ignored his implied threat. 'Go flatter Fiona,' she threw over her shoulder as she headed for the stairs.

'Jealous?' he sneered.

'Of you?' Kate turned to him with a withering look. 'She can have you with my blessing. About which I shall say more later. After you bring yourself to say goodnight to your friends.'

CHAPTER TWO

KATE was in the bathroom creaming the make-up from her face when she heard the last of the guests leave, their departure enlivened by a stream of jocose comments from Scott. He had undoubtedly excused her absence by saying she had a headache. Tomorrow the headache would become a migraine. Everyone on the cruise would say, 'Poor Kate!' and not give a damn. She would only be a wet blanket anyway with her need to stay fully clothed. No matter what Scott said, she would not go. Enough was enough. In fact it was more than enough.

The front door closed and Scott's footsteps thudded up the stairs. When she walked back into the bedroom he was undressing. He stripped well. He always had. Kate felt not one flicker of desire. The strong, muscular body might as well have been a statue.

He threw her a surly look. 'Well, what are you sulking about? I thought you were doing quite well for yourself with Alex Dalton.'

'I'm not going with you tomorrow, Scott.'

'Like hell you're not! This is the big one, Kate. I'm cracking into it at last and I'm not going to let you wreck it for me.'

'It has nothing to do with me.'

The handsome face turned ugly. 'You stupid bitch! Haven't you learnt yet how a deal gets done? Nothing's ever straightforward. I need you and you're coming with me and there'll be no argument about it.'

'You don't need me. You haven't needed me for a long time, if you ever needed me at all,' Kate replied heatedly.

He made a grimace of disgust. 'Don't start on all that self-pity guff again. I can't stomach it tonight. You're coming with me and that's that.'

'Why should I? Just why the hell should I? It's not as if you're trying to present a façade of marital bliss. You don't really want me with you.'

He had sat down to remove his socks and he threw her a sardonic look over his shoulder. 'It's not what I want. It's what he wants. If you weren't such a buttoned-up case of arrested sexuality you'd know that Dalton wants to gobble you up.' He gave a sarcastic laugh. 'Must be the carrot hair. Nothing else about you looks hot.'

'That's so typical of you, Scott,' Kate retorted with blistering scorn. 'You have to reduce everything to the lowest level. Alex Dalton . . .'

'Alex Dalton came here tonight for one reason and one reason only.' He stood up and lazily stretched his back muscles before swinging around and jabbing a finger in her direction. 'And you were that reason.'

'Oh, don't be ridiculous!'

'Ridiculous, am I?' he scoffed, then shook his head knowingly. 'Our friend, Dalton, is a very cagey bird. He very pointedly admired the photograph of you in my office and then remarked that he wouldn't make a decision on our deal until Monday, that he'd like the weekend to consider it more fully. He looked again at the photograph and very reluctantly put it back on my desk. Now, you might choose to be deaf, dumb and blind, but I'm an old hand at picking up vibes. My dinner invitation was snapped up and he gave you his very exclusive attention all night. And tomorrow, my dear wife, you are going to be all sweetness and light aboard his yacht. Do I make myself clear?'

'Crystal!' she spat at him, boiling over with rage. 'You're nothing but a pimp! How dare you think you can prostitute me like that!'

'Oh, for God's sake!' he snarled. 'I'm not asking you to go to bed with him. Just give out a little, make him feel appreciated.'

Kate's anger was intensified by a hot wave of humiliation. Some of Alex Dalton's remarks scorched across her mind and she felt nauseous as their full meaning hit her. 'He doesn't want me, you fool!' she bit out with fiery contempt. 'It simply amuses him to manipulate people. It's all a game to him, setting off the moves and watching people react. That was what he was doing tonight and that's what he'll be doing tomorrow. You're nothing but a puppet to him and he'll only buy that invention if he thinks it'll work for him. You can supply him with amusement if you want to, but I won't.'

'Yes, you will, Kate,' Scott grated out, rounding the bed purposefully. He gripped her upper arms, his fingers digging into the soft flesh. 'You'll lower that snooty nose and you'll smile and be nice, be very nice, or I'll whip that frigid body of yours into submission right now.'

'What's the matter, Scott? Fiona not satisfying you?' she jabbed at him, acid dripping off her tongue.

He shook her angrily. 'We'll leave Fiona out of this. You don't know what you're talking about.'

'I'm talking about a divorce.'

The words were out, shocking them both for a moment. His hold on her slackened.

'You don't mean that, Kate. You're my wife,' he declared tersely.

'Nice of you to remember. I had the impression that Fiona had taken my place and you considered me little more than a whore you could offer around to prospective clients. That finishes us, Scott. I'm leaving you and I'm leaving you tomorrow.'

'No!' he said vehemently.

But Kate knew she would. The decision had been growing in her for a long time and now it had been made. He saw the hard decision in her eyes and his tough stance crumpled.

'You can't, Kate,' he pleaded, his hands running up her shoulders to cup her face. 'You're my wife.'

She wrenched herself out of his grasp and paced away from him. 'Your wife!' she echoed derisively. 'More like a marketable asset. I clean your house, I cook, I bring in an income, I look reasonably decorative, but when did you last love and cherish me, Scott? You wouldn't even let me have a baby.'

'All right! We'll have a child if you're so desperate for one,' he said grudgingly.

'I don't want one any more. I don't want anything from you any more. I just want to leave you,' she said dully.

He came up behind her, sliding his arms

around her waist and pulling her back against him.

'Don't!' she said with a weary sigh.

He ignored her. One hand spread across the slight curve of her stomach, the other pushed inside the low V-neckline of her nightie and began caressing her breasts. 'You're just upset, Kate, making mountains out of molehills,' he murmured against her ear. 'Let me relax you.'

She did not move. She waited to see if she felt anything, if his lovemaking could awaken any spark in her. There was only a vast, cold emptiness which Scott's hands could not reach.

'It won't work, Scott. Not this time. It's over between us. I don't love you and I don't want you,' she stated flatly. She removed his hands from her body and swung around to face him. 'I won't live with you any more.'

His chin came up aggressively and resentment flared into his eyes. 'So! You picked a fine time to slap a divorce in my face. You wait until I need you, really need you, and then you pull the mat out from under my feet. How selfish can you get!'

The accusation stunned Kate for a moment. It was unbelievable in the situation Scott had engineered. Yet nothing about Scott was unbelievable. He was capable of every dirty trick in the book. Kate was not blind any more. Her eyes were wide open and she looked at him contemptuously.

'I don't care. I don't care if you end up a millionaire or land in the gutter. I won't be any part of it. I'm walking out of your life and I'm making a new life for myself.'

A cunning gleam snaked into his eyes. 'What if I won't give you a divorce?'

'You don't have to give me one. I'll get one automatically, simply by living apart from you for one year. Do you think I'm ignorant, Scott?'

'What if I don't leave you alone? I could fix some witnesses to say we'd spent a night together. I could easily jam up your clean, tidy plans. You might find that divorce more difficult than you think, Kate.'

'You . . .' Fury gorged her throat at his dog-in-the-manger attitude.

He held up his hands in mock protest. 'Now, now, Kate. Let's talk reasonably. You've made your point. You want a divorce. I'm prepared to let you go with no hassles on one condition, and that condition, my darling wife, is that you act a very willing part tomorrow on Alex Dalton's yacht.'

He was mad. Kate stared at him disbelievingly. Scott had no conception of Alex Dalton's character. It would make no whit of difference to Scott's prospects of success if she accompanied him on the cruise. Suddenly she realised it did not matter to her what Alex Dalton thought either. His cynical amusement could simply wash over her. She could smile and be responsive on the surface, pretending a friendliness which would buy her freedom. That was all she had to remember to make the act easy. After tomorrow all those people would cease to exist for her. They did not matter, not even Scott. She looked at him and he was already a stranger.

'All right. It's a deal,' she said slowly.

His eyes narrowed with suspicion. 'You'd better play fair, Kate. I'll be watching you.'

'I'll do my bit to charm Alex Dalton, never fear. You'll have no reason to complain on that score. But what happens in your office on Monday morning is out of my hands. Don't blame me if your strategy doesn't work.'

'It'll work,' he said confidently. 'Where are you going?' he added as she walked towards the hallway.

'Not even a king-size bed puts enough distance between us tonight,' she replied coldly. 'I'll sleep in the guest room.'

'Suit yourself.' He shrugged and headed for the en-suite bathroom.

Kate knew his manner held a lot of bravado. If she had showed any softness he would have been all over her like a rash. It was not that he wanted her. He just hated losing. Anything.

She did not sleep well. Her mind was churning with all the things she would have to do in effecting a separation from Scott. Even so she awoke feeling surprisingly carefree. It was still quite early. She had forgotten to pull down the blind and the morning sunshine was streaming into the room. She slid out of bed, remade it and went down to the kitchen to make herself a cup of coffee.

There was work to be done if she was leaving tomorrow. All the good tableware from last night's party had to be put away and the linen put through the washing-machine. She would leave the house tidy and clean. There was nothing she wanted to take with her except her clothes. Scott could keep everything else. He had chosen most of their possessions and would have the sole responsibility for making the outstanding payments. Kate wanted a clean break. She was in the laundry when Scott made his appearance. He was already dressed in T-shirt and jeans.

'Why didn't you wake me?' he growled. 'We'll be late if we don't get a move on. Leave that and get ready to go.'

Not wishing to cause any friction Kate obeyed. She washed and changed into white slacks and a blue and white pin-striped shirt. The long sleeves had white cuffs and although collarless, the neckline was trimmed with white and buttons ran down to just below her breasts. She tidied her hair into a chignon and grabbed a wide-brimmed straw hat, trimmed with a blue and white scarf. Normally she wore sandals with this outfit but after a moment's hesitation she slipped on a pair of navy canvas joggers. They were more suitable for walking on a rocking deck.

'Ready?' Scott demanded impatiently.

'Yes, I was just coming,' she replied, straightening up and swinging around.

'My God! You look like a bloody nun!' he accused angrily. 'Is this what you call playing fair?'

Kate flushed and stood her ground. 'I'm not getting sunburnt for anyone, Scott. You know how vulnerable I am.'

'I'm not asking you to get sunburnt, but just look at yourself. Go on! Look in the mirror!' He grabbed her hand and dragged her over to the large mirror on the dressing-table. 'Does that look like a woman who wants to interest a man?' He pulled out her hair-pins and raked his fingers roughly through the long wavy tresses. 'That's a start. Now put some make-up on and brighten yourself up. You look pasty.'

Kate did not argue. It was not worth arguing about. Her hands shook a little as she applied some blue eye-shadow and darkened her lashes with mascara. She added a soft coral lipstick and then brushed out her hair, fluffing it around her shoulders in a gleaming red-gold mass.

'Will that do?' she asked, a sarcastic edge on her tongue.

He eyed her critically. 'That shirt is too prim and proper. Undo the buttons.'

Still clinging to her temper Kate undid the top three buttons.

'All of them,' he insisted.

'Like hell!' she muttered resentfully. 'I'm not going as some walking invitation.'

'You'll go as I say or the divorce is off.'

She glared at him, ready to fight, but the challenging gleam in his eyes told her he relished a fight. With her chin lifted defiantly she flicked open the rest of her buttons.

'Satisfied?'

'A bit of honey on your tongue won't go astray,' he retorted harshly. He glanced at his watch. 'Damn! We're running late now. Come on,' he urged, pushing her ahead of him. 'And just remember I'll have no scruples about dirtying up your divorce. Do your bit and I'll leave you alone.'

Kate sat in mutinous silence as they drove along. Scott prattled on, ignoring her mood.

'He has a house with its own private anchorage at Double Bay, lucky devil. Must have cost a packet. The yacht has a permanent crew too. He can just give the word and everything's ready for him to sail whenever he likes. That's rich, really rich, believe me. To think he had it made at my age. He's sold franchises for his products in half the countries around the world. You've got to be lucky. It's not enough to be smart. You've got to have the luck too. Be in the right place at the right time with the right product. I've got it this time. I know it in my bones. And he's the right man to get it moving. If he'll just sign on the dotted line I've got it made.' He threw her a triumphant look. 'Are you listening to me, Kate?'

'Yes,' she answered tersely.

'Look! If you can keep him sweet I'll even give you a piece of the action, keep you afloat while you look around for whatever you want. I mean it, Kate. I'll make it worth your while,' he said eagerly.

She disdained to answer. Scott was a pimp, already offering payment for services she had no intention of giving. She would be pleasant to Alex Dalton but the unbuttoned shirt was firmly buttoned as far as she was concerned. He could think what he liked but there was not going to be any action.

'Did you hear me?' Scott threw at her irritably.

'I heard you.'

'Well?'

'Well what? I said I'd be nice to him.'

She felt his hard scrutiny but looked straight ahead. He lapsed into silence until they pulled up outside a high brick wall.

'He obviously likes his privacy,' Scott commented as they alighted from the station wagon.

'Through that gate,' he directed. 'Alex said there was a path leading down past the house to the jetty. Hurry up, Kate. From the look of the cars everyone else is here.'

Scott hustled her forward. The house was split-level, spilling downwards to the rocks below. It looked reasonably modern and the landscaping of the grounds was obviously recent. The sandstone steps were wide and shallow, making it an easy walk to the jetty. The dinghy was being held there by a pleasant-faced young man.

'Mr and Mrs Andrews?' he asked politely. At Scott's breezy acknowledgment he gestured for them to climb down. 'You first, Mr Andrews. I'll help Mrs Andrews down while you steady the dinghy.'

'I'm afraid we're a bit late,' Scott said apologetically.

'No problem. Mr Dalton's not in any hurry. It's only a pleasure cruise.'

'It's a big yacht,' Scott commented appreciatively as his gaze took in the sleek white lines of it.

'Mr Dalton spends a lot of time on it,' the crewman grinned. 'The communications equipment is fantastic. Instant radio, telephone and telex contact can be established with anywhere in the world from anywhere at sea. He can run his business from the yacht.'

'That's the way to live. Must cost him a hell of a lot to run,' Scott mused.

The young man's grin widened. 'I reckon so. You all right there, Mrs Andrews?'

'Yes, thank you.'

Kate was grimly hanging on to her hat as the breeze whipped long strands of her hair across her face. Fortunately her sun-glasses kept it out of her eyes. She silently cursed Scott for insisting she wear her hair loose.

'Almost there,' the lad said cheerfully, and indeed his strong rowing had made short work of the distance.

Alex Dalton was on hand to greet them as they climbed on board the yacht.

Scott started with his usual glib chatter. 'Sorry to hold you up. Kate's fault. You know what women are like.'

Alex Dalton looked straight at Kate. 'I'm only glad you came.'

The remark was uncomfortably personal and was meant to be so. He had deliberately cut Scott out. Kate was forcibly reminded of the hard ruthlessness she had seen in his eyes last night. He took her hand and smiled a tigerish smile of satisfaction. 'I've organised a table in the shade for you. It's protected from sun and wind so you won't have any more trouble with a hat. You can leave it off.'

He had obviously watched their approach. That look in his eyes and the assumed possession of her hand sent a prickle of apprehension up Kate's spine. She had not believed Scott's estimate of Alex Dalton but a sudden doubt ripped through her mind. Scott sent her a warning glance and her reflexive move to detach herself from Alex Dalton wilted into passiveness. Holding hands was harmless enough.

He led them to the aft end of the main deck where there was a partly covered sunlounge.

Cane armchairs, footstools and tables were in the shaded area while air-beds provided comfortable relaxation for those wishing to sun themselves.

The same company from last night was sprawled around and they all chided the late-comers good-naturedly. Kate's gaze swept around the women. Jan Lister wore a tank-top and bermuda shorts which were highly unflattering to her wide thighs. Kate smiled at her. Jan might have no clothes sense but of the women present she had by far the nicest nature. Wendy Jessell was in a yellow towelling playsuit which showed off her dark tan and accentuated her fluffy blonde hair. Kate's eyes skated over Fiona Chardway. She was stretched out on an airbed at the far end of the deck, soaking up the sun. The voluptuous display of oiled skin was minimally interrupted by a red string bikini. Her long, black hair was rolled into a loose chignon at the top of her head and Kate wondered ironically if Scott would remove her hairpins.

Scott made straight for Fiona, dropping down beside her and giving her a wolfish smile. Alex Dalton drew Kate towards two deck-chairs which were set further away from the others. Apparently he was determined on having her to himself. After seeing her comfortably settled into one of the chairs he dropped into the other and signalled to a hovering deck-hand.

'What would you like to drink?'

'A lemonade will be fine,' she smiled, trying to cover her unease.

He made a gesture towards Scott as he relayed the order. '... And look after Mr Andrews. Don't let him want for anything.'

The pointed remark made Kate even more uneasy. She made a few stilted comments about the weather until the drinks came. She was surprised to see pineapple juice put in front of Alex Dalton. He grinned disarmingly.

'I like my own products and I rarely drink alcohol before evening. It fuzzes the mind.'

And you don't want a fuzzy mind today, Kate added privately. Scott was a babe in the woods compared to this man. Alex Dalton was deep and dangerous and she hated the necessity of playing along with him.

The yacht got under way and Alex Dalton was kept busy answering questions about its performances. Once he stood up and moved to the railing to explain something to Bob Chardway. Kate took the opportunity to re-appraise the man.

Last night he had seemed chunky, overweight, but the navy shorts and cotton-knit shirt showed there was no excess flesh anywhere. His arms and legs were thicker in girth than that of the other men's but it was all strong muscle. Strong and sturdy, like a tree-trunk, Kate mused, and just about as immovable.

His dark head suddenly whipped around, the sharp, blue eyes slicing to her, showing an awareness which made her flush for staring at him. His gaze dropped momentarily to her gaping neckline and her embarrassment deepened. A darted glance at Scott showed his attention was all on Fiona and Kate breathed a sigh of relief.

'Jack, here, will answer all your questions,' Alex Dalton said abruptly. He handed Bob over to the man who had served them drinks. Then he was striding back to her, lowering himself into his chair and throwing her a rueful smile. 'There are definite disadvantages in playing host. I plan to be a lazy one. You're looking very delectable today, Mary Kathleen.'

'Thank you,' she murmured, inwardly cringing from that word, 'delectable'. It recalled Scott's words of last night all too vividly and she did not want to give them credit.

His eyes crinkled with amusement. 'What shall we talk about?'

'Whatever you like.'

'Oh, we are so amenable today,' he said with lilting mockery. 'A change of scenery, no social pressures, and you are sweetly soft.'

He trailed a caressing finger down her arm and Kate froze, gripping the armrest tightly as little shivers of revulsion crawled over her skin. Had she misjudged the man, she questioned wildly. No, she reasoned more calmly. He was playing a cynical game with her, seeing how far she would let him go. She heard Bob ask a question which Jack could not answer and impulsively invited their attention.

'I can tell you, Bob,' she called out.

They turned, looking at her expectantly, and the intimacy Alex Dalton had introduced was effectively broken.

'It was called Pinchgut Island because hardened criminals were marooned there in the early convict days. There was no prison built at that time so they were isolated on the island and only given a small amount of rations to exist on. Thus Pinchgut. It wasn't turned into a fort until the early 1840s and then it became Fort Denison.'

'Why did they bother turning it into a fort?' Bob questioned. 'I realise it's an ideal position for protecting old Sydney Cove but who was going to attack a measly little colony?'

'There was a rumour of war breaking out between Britain and America and there were French and American squadrons sailing the Pacific. The colonists were a long way from home and they wanted protection from anyone sailing in and taking over,' Kate explained. Then eager to retain their interest she added, 'It was quite funny really. The British Colonial Office sent out the guns for the fort but neglected to send anyone to man them. The soldiers here didn't have the expertise. The guns were mounted on the batteries but they had no one to fire them if they'd ever been needed.'

'Typical!' Bob nodded knowingly. 'Thanks, Kate. You're a mine of information,' he added and turned back to the railing.

Kate sighed, disappointed that his interest had lapsed. She was left alone with Alex Dalton again.

'That's an unusual piece of knowledge,' he remarked, looking at her quizzically.

She shrugged. 'My employer is a historian. If you'd typed as many notes on early Australian history as I have, you wouldn't wonder at the odd bit of knowledge sticking.'

'You must find it interesting work.'

'Yes, it is really. Sometimes fascinating.'

Much to her surprise and relief he drew her out on the subject. Kate gradually relaxed, her face becoming animated as she related some of the odd coincidences which had turned up in the young colony. He in turn told her some unusual historical snippets about the West Indian colonies which he had visited in his travels. He was an amusing raconteur and Kate really began to enjoy his company, warming to his more open humour. She laughed at his amusing stories and was even more amused to see Scott's occasional glances of satisfaction. She had her elbow propped on the table, her cheek cupped in her hand, her eyes sparkling with interest when Alex suddenly broke off speaking and eyed her speculatively.

'Do you know whom you remind me of?'

She wrinkled her nose at him, unconsciously flirtatious. 'No, tell me.'

He leaned forward, lifting the hair from her shoulder and letting it run through his fingers. 'Botticelli's Venus rising from the sea. You have the same shade of red-gold hair. There's a good print of it hanging below deck. Come down and I'll show you.'

His hand slid down from her shoulder to her elbow, lifting her up as he stood. Kate rose stiffly and reluctantly, not wanting to leave the company of the others. Her eyes flicked to Scott who nodded at her, a complacent little smile on his lips. Kate gritted her teeth as Alex Dalton steered her to the gangway. His grip on her elbow was too purposeful for her liking. Had he mistaken her manner for encouragement, she asked herself worriedly. She paused at the bottom of the stairs and looked around the luxuriously furnished saloon. It was all turquoise and green, cool and inviting with comfortable sofas and chairs. There were several pictures on the walls but no Venus rising from any sea.

Alex Dalton's bulk was behind her, suddenly threatening. His hand rested on her hip. 'Through here,' he murmured, almost pushing her towards a door to the side of the stairs.

He leaned past her and opened it. Kate dragged her feet as he propelled her forward. It was a stateroom. She stopped dead as her eyes fixed on the large double bed which dominated her mind as well as the room. She did not bother looking at the walls for pictures. She flinched as strong hands covered the bruises left by Scott.

'Oh God, no,' she breathed.

The next instant she was twisting away from him, backing across the room, her eyes fiercely rejecting him. He made no attempt to hold her or follow her. She came up against a wall and stood there, hugging herself protectively, her hands moving instinctively to rub the sore spots on her arms. She faced him with proud defiance.

'The game stops here, Mr Dalton. I won't play it. Not for any price.'

He nodded, and surprisingly there was a soft compassion in his eyes. 'I didn't think you would, Mary Kathleen, but I wanted to know.'

CHAPTER THREE

HIS gaze slid to the agitated movement of her hands, then rose again sharply. 'Do those long sleeves cover bruises? Did Scott force you into this by beating you?'

'No,' she denied quickly.

For a big man he moved like a panther. He grabbed the opened neckline of her shirt and pulled it down over one shoulder. The purpled marks left by Scott's fingers stood out as damning evidence on her white skin.

'I bruise easily,' she mumbled, flushing with embarrassment. 'Please let it go.'

His expression was grim as he silently adjusted her clothing. He very deliberately did up her buttons, finishing at the throat. Then his hands cupped her face, forcing her to look at him. His eyes were softly apologetic.

'Please forgive me.'

She stared at him, too confused by his actions to find any answer.

He sighed and dropped his hands. 'God damn the bastard! I didn't think he'd stoop to that.' He turned away and waved a hand towards a chair. 'Sit down. You can relax now.'

Kate did not move, still too shocked to comprehend what he could mean by this sudden switch. 'I'd rather return to the deck.'

'And spoil the whole show?' he threw at her mockingly. 'We both know that your husband expects me to enjoy your favours. That takes a certain amount of time, Mary Kathleen, and I don't intend him to have any doubts on the matter.' He dropped on to the bed, stretching out full length with his hands behind his head. 'What was the price?'

Kate closed her eyes. Never in her life had she felt such dreadful humiliation. The ugly bluntness of Alex Dalton's words hammered it in, soiling her with Scott's corruption.

'I'm sorry. I've been rough on you, haven't I? Please sit down. You're quite safe with me. I've never taken an unwilling woman in my life.'

The voice was gentler, softly persuasive. She peered at him uncertainly from beneath her lashes, then decided she might as well accept his invitation. He was right, however brutally he expressed it. Scott would not be pleased to see her return so soon. She took the chair he had indicated. It was soft and comfortable and she sank into it gratefully. Her nerves had been badly shaken in the last few minutes.

'Your husband must be pretty desperate to try and use you. He's also a fool to think he can manipulate me.'

The dry observation rankled. 'Then why did you go along with him?'

He stared up at the timber ceiling for long, silent moments. When he answered it was in a voice of weary cynicism. 'I was out of patience with people trying to use me. Scott hit a nerve which was already pulsing rather painfully.'

'So you thought you would teach him a lesson,' Kate muttered, thinking how grossly Scott had misjudged his mark.

The hard blue eyes sliced to her and his mouth twisted with irony. 'And you. I thought you could do with a lesson too.'

'Why me? What had I ever done to you?' she demanded resentfully.

He looked at her in an odd, reflective way, as if not quite seeing her but an image in his mind, and the image did not please him. 'There's a photograph of you in Scott's office. It seemed an innocent face, radiant with love and laughter.'

She sighed and made a wry grimace. 'It was taken just before we were married.'

'Yes. You're not that girl any more,' he commented bluntly and turned his face to the ceiling again. 'I was looking at your photograph, thinking Scott was a lucky man to have such a woman as his wife, and he suddenly started selling you. It curdled my stomach. I thought, here's another beautiful face which hides a rotten soul. Women make such fools of men.'

There was such harsh contempt in his voice that Kate's hackles rose. 'Men do their share of fooling women,' she declared bitterly.

He turned his gaze back to her and this time his eyes were keenly concentrated. 'Yes. You're a very disillusioned woman. You surprised me. You weren't what I expected at all. The image was right, beautiful, an accomplished hostess, no children and no intention of having any. The company was right. Everyone there was on the make. But you were wrong.

'I kept getting the wrong answers when I probed. And you blocked or retreated from every advance. It was an odd situation. The signals from Scott were positive, but yours were almost

too negative. I couldn't make up my mind whether
you were handing me a genuine rejection or a very
subtle challenge.' He frowned in puzzlement.
'Surely Scott had worded you up on me?'

Kate returned a sour smile. 'Scott always tells
me to be nice to his clients. He was only watching
you last night. Your . . . interest in me encouraged
his idea. It wasn't until everyone had gone that
. . . that . . .' Her voice faltered as she remembered
the ugly scene which had followed.

'That he applied pressure,' Alex Dalton
finished contemptuously.

'Yes,' she whispered, looking at him with
bleak, wintry eyes.

'I am sorry, you know,' he said gently. 'What
pressure did he use? Violence?'

She dropped her lashes over the sudden well of
tears and shook her head.

'Not violence. What then?'

She could not speak. The softness in his voice
and the unexpected sympathy after nerve-
snapping tension, were wreaking havoc on her
control.

'Mary Kathleen?'

She bit her lips and swallowed hard, fighting
the constriction in her throat. The bed creaked
and she looked up with startled tear-washed eyes.

'It's all right. I'm not going to attack you.' He
was sitting on the edge of the bed. With a heavy
sigh he leaned forward and rested his elbows on
his knees. One hand raked the short, thick hair.
'Why do you stay with him? He's blatantly
unfaithful to you. He certainly doesn't care about
you if he's prepared to push you into bed with
me. He won't even give you the children you

want.' He shot her a sharp look beneath his frown. 'I did get that right, didn't I?'

'Yes. I wanted children,' she answered jerkily and drew in a deep breath to steady herself.

He raised an eyebrow. 'Not any more?'

'With Scott as their father?' she retorted bitterly.

'Then leave him. He's no good to you.'

'I'm going to. This . . . this was the end, you see. That he'd use me like a . . . like a . . .' She could not bring herself to use the word. She looked down at her wedding rings and twisted them around her finger. Total disillusionment shadowed her face. 'I was brought up to respect marriage vows. Promises are forever. I kept trying . . . hoping that it could be different . . . but the hope ran out last night. I told him I wanted a divorce. Then . . . then . . . he said . . .'

'I was the price for letting you go free.'

The savage disgust in the words startled her. She glanced up at him questioningly. His mouth had thinned into grim lines and the hard ruthlessness was back in his eyes.

'I'll teach that bastard a lesson he'll never forget tomorrow.' Then he frowned and made an irritable sound. 'No. That might rebound on you.' He sucked in a deep breath and let it out slowly, shaking his head at her. 'Oh, Mary Kathleen! What are you doing in this nest of vipers?'

It provoked a shaky smile from her. 'I thought I was in the Garden of Eden when I married Scott, but I guess I married the snake.'

He nodded and returned her smile. 'And I guess I'll have to let him slither away.'

'I would be grateful if you'd just let the matter drop.'

'And you have little enough to be grateful to me for. When you stepped on board this morning I was going to . . .' He saw the sharp recoil in her eyes and gave a light shrug. 'Well, you were dressed for the part.'

'I know,' she sighed. 'I didn't care. I thought Scott was wrong about you. It didn't seem to me last night that you . . . that you fancied me.'

His eyes suddenly gleamed with self-mockery. 'Oh, I fancied you all right.'

She flushed. 'But . . . but you weren't going to make love to me. It was all a game, wasn't it?'

'When I play games, Mary Kathleen, I play them to the hilt. I wouldn't call it making love, but yes, I would've taken you to bed. That was part of the scenario . . . and you do have beautiful skin.'

The admired skin burnt red with embarrassment as she recoiled from his cynicism. 'I don't like you, Mr Dalton,' she said coldly.

'No, I don't suppose you do,' he replied equably. A faint smile curved his lips. 'But I like you, Mary Kathleen. It's been a fascinating morning all told. I very quickly perceived that the situation was not what it seemed. Despite your encouraging exterior, each time I touched you your instinctive impulse was to withdraw. Then you'd look at Scott and become passive. You rushed into speech too nervously. All the vibrations were wrong, as they'd been last night, only I was too sceptical then to give them much credit. It was only when I dropped the pressure that you relaxed and responded. I enjoyed our conversation, Mary Kathleen.'

'I was enjoying it too,' she admitted ruefully but her eyes still condemned him. 'If you'd already decided you were wrong about me, why did you spoil it with this?'

His smile turned into a wry grimace. 'There was the remote possibility that the game was still on. You had reduced it to your terms, you see. We were talking as equals.' A gentle warmth came into his eyes. 'And I wanted you.'

She closed her eyes and shook her head, rejecting everything about him.

'Tell me what you're going to do, now that you're leaving Scott. Go back to your family?' he asked softly.

She had told him too much already. She wondered what had possessed her to be so open with this man. He could use the knowledge against her if the whim took him. He was dangerous.

'Come now. You might as well talk to me. We haven't been here nearly long enough to suggest intimacy has taken place.'

She looked at him accusingly. 'I thought you said you weren't pursuing this game.'

'Your husband will go easier on you if we pretend.'

Relief softened her resistance and there seemed no harm in talking of the future. 'That's ... thoughtful of you. No, I won't be going back to my family. My mother died when I was fourteen. Dad married again and they have a young family now. They have their own life to live, apart from

which, they live in Tasmania. I've got a job here
and I have to stay to get my divorce.'

He nodded. 'Any friends to lean on?'

She threw him a derisive look.

'No friends.'

'Only like the ones upstairs. They're Scott's
friends. I want to cut free anyhow. I've had
enough of . . .' She sighed despondently. 'You
don't want to hear this.'

'Yes I do.'

Her eyes mocked his assertion.

'I'm interested in you,' he insisted.

'I don't want you interested in me, Mr Dalton,'
she said bluntly.

'Alex. You can't go to bed with me and call me
Mr Dalton. It's too inconsistent. You have to
play your part, Mary Kathleen, and you'd better
start practising.'

She conceded the point, 'Alex, then.'

'Good girl!'

He grinned. It was a friendly, open grin which
gave his face a magnetic charm. Kate privately
acknowledged that most women would find him
very attractive.

'And in the interests of consistency . . .' he
picked up a small box of tissues from the bedside table and tossed it to her, '. . . wipe off your
lipstick, You don't even look kissed, let alone
ravished.'

She could not repress a little smile. 'This is
crazy. I won't be able to carry it off.'

'You don't have to. Just keep on being nice to
me as you were this morning. I'll find an
opportunity to tell Scott what "a marvellous
wife" he has. And the crazy part is, Mary

Kathleen, I'll be telling the truth.'

She stopped rubbing the tissue over her mouth and frowned at him. 'What do you mean by that?' she demanded suspiciously.

He laughed and stretched out on the bed again. 'Let me tell you, women who keep their marriage vows are few and far between. I think that rates a "marvellous".'

'You really are a very cynical man, Alex Dalton.'

'Most probably.' He smiled. 'You are no longer an innocent, Mary Kathleen, yet you have a purity of soul which I like very much. An honesty which one meets all too rarely.'

It suddenly struck Kate that this whole conversation had been strangely honest. Ever since they had entered this room there had been no pretence between them. She did not like Alex Dalton's cynicism but at least she no longer had to fence with him. She could talk to him directly. He understood.

It was ironic that his intrusion into their lives had brought a change for the better. Her marriage was finished and Alex Dalton had been the catalyst which finished it. 'I'm glad you accepted Scott's invitation,' she remarked thoughtfully. 'I might've gone on wasting a few more years.'

There was suddenly a discomforting warmth in his eyes. 'Do you know, I find you the most attractive woman I've ever met.'

The compliment was not welcome. Not in this situation. She evaded his disturbing gaze and looked down at her hands. The tissue she had been holding was a crumpled ball. 'I think . . . I think we've been down here long enough,' she said tightly.

'I doubt that I could have done you justice in so short a time.'

He was teasing her. She made no response. After a short silence he sighed and the bed creaked again.

'Forgive me. My tongue runs away from me occasionally. Let's be friends.'

She glanced up and could not help responding to his whimsical smile. 'For the rest of the day,' she agreed.

'Well, that's a start.'

He stood up and she followed suit.

'Just follow my lead. We'll be relaxed and comfortable. Okay?'

'I'll try.' She hesitated, finding his name and the words difficult. 'Alex . . . thank you for . . . for . . .'

'For not being quite the rotter you thought I was?'

'Something like that.'

'I do like to surprise people,' he said sardonically. 'Come on. We'll go and surprise a few others.'

They reappeared on deck. Speculative eyes turned on to them and slid away, but Alex was master of the situation. He settled Kate and himself, then deliberately drew the others around, promoting an easy atmosphere with light quips and breezy conversation. Kate could not help smiling. He really was a clever operator. She caught the question in Scott's eyes but gave him no answer, taking savage satisfaction in keeping him guessing.

The yacht rode at anchor while they had lunch. Tables were set up with a wide selection of cold meats and salad and Alex invited everyone to help themselves. They were just settling down with loaded plates when the Manly hydrofoil skimmed past, its wash lightly rocking them.

'By God! That's really travelling,' Bob Chardway remarked in awe as the hydrofoil zoomed up the harbour towards the shining sails of the Opera House which dominated Benelong Point.

'It works on the same principle as a jet-plane, pushing air behind it,' Alex commented.

'Sure leaves the old ferries for dead,' Bob grinned. 'What is it? Fifteen minutes for the Manly trip instead of an hour?'

'Something like that.'

'It's not the same though,' Jan Lister chimed in. 'I prefer the old ferry where you can sit out on deck and enjoy churning across the harbour. You can't even see out of the hydrofoil windows when you're sitting down, not unless you're about seven feet tall. I reckon the designer made a terrible error there.'

'It was built for speed, not for tourists,' Terry Jessell said derisively. 'Think of the time commuters save. I bet they'd prefer to have another half-hour in bed than look at scenery they've observed a thousand times before.'

'Oh, you men! You're all philistines! All you can think of is your creature comforts,' Jan said disgustedly.

'What else, when you're such a comfortable creature, Jan,' Scott grinned. 'Still, we're enjoying the scenery today.'

'Among other things,' Fiona Chardway put in

silkily. She threw a knowing look at Kate before favouring Alex with her provocative gaze. 'Could we have a swim after lunch before we get under way again?'

'If you're prepared to brave the sharks,' he smiled.

Fiona's lips quirked sensuously. 'There are sharks everywhere, Alex. I'm game to risk it.'

The husky intonation of her voice reinforced the invitation in her eyes. Kate watched curiously to see how Alex would react to the offer because it was an offer, only thinly disguised.

His smile took on a sardonic twist. 'You're a braver person than I am, my dear. I'm very discriminating in the use of my body. I don't cast it around for anything to take.'

It was a beautiful put-down. Kate had to swallow hard to keep her glee from showing. Fiona's mouth tightened. Green eyes sparked hostility at Kate and then they were smiling seductively at Scott.

'You'll come with me, won't you, darling?'

There was a momentary hesitation and then a lascivious grin spread across his face. 'Sure. Why not?'

'You're a fool, Fiona,' Bob Chardway muttered wearily.

She turned on him with a scornful look. 'Just because you're too bloated with alcohol to fancy any exercise, don't start picking on me, Bob.'

'And you're an even worse fool, Scott,' Bob added carelessly before burying his face in a tankard of beer.

Alex deftly veered the conversation on to

water-sports, surfing, skiing, board-riding, the Australian domination in the recent World Championships in Hawaii. The meal dragged on, washed down by chilled white wines. Fiona and Scott lazed back in the sun, their bodies glistening with oil. Sometime during the morning Scott had removed his shirt and jeans and the brief swimming trunks were as revealing as Fiona's bikini. Physically they were well-matched and Kate wondered if they would get together after she left. It did not look as if Bob Chardway would care. He was steadily drinking himself under the table.

'We're going in,' Fiona suddenly announced.

'As you like,' Alex nodded. 'I wouldn't advise swimming too far from the yacht.'

There was a short, watching silence as they clambered over the side and dropped into the water. Fiona squealed and Scott laughed. The conversation on deck picked up again. It was some fifteen minutes later that Terry Jessell started up, his gaze turned to the water.

'What the devil is Scott doing out there? He's past the buoy, the stupid idiot.' He quickly moved to the railing and yelled for Scott to come back in.

Both the Listers stood up to look and Jan threw a cynical look back at Kate. 'Fiona's floating near the buoy. I bet she challenged him to a race and then didn't bother.'

'The hydrofoil! My God!' Terry gasped and began waving frantically, screaming at the top of his lungs.

Fear sliced through Kate and she ran to the railing, pushing past the others, staring in horror as the hydrofoil whipped over the water in a straight line for Scott. He had seen it. His arms and legs were thrashing in an effort to swim out of its path. It was coming too fast. He stopped swimming. His face turned towards the imminent threat. His arms reached out and then his body arced briefly as he dived. His legs kicked and disappeared. Kate held her breath and prayed wildly for his safety. The hydrofoil raced past, its skipper unaware of any small, human obstacle. Her eyes searched the waves, willing Scott's head to bob up. Jan Lister screamed and Kate was abruptly swung around and pressed against a broad chest.

'Don't look,' Alex muttered grimly. One strong hand kept her head averted as cries of distress jangled in her ears. 'He didn't make it.'

It was a heavy sigh and his arm tightened its hold, supporting her against collapse. She sagged, too weak with shock to even think of resisting. She vaguely heard him issuing orders and then he was half-carrying her down to the saloon. He settled her on a sofa, propping cushions around her. Her head was whirling with horror. Her whole body was trembling uncontrollably. There was the sound of footsteps thudding down the stairs, a subdued mumble of voices, a sense of shock pervading everything. A hand stroked her forehead and she focused on the glass near her face.

'Drink this. It'll help.'

Her eyelashes fluttered up and she looked blankly at the big man until her reeling mind told her it was Alex and she could depend on him. She sipped the brandy he handed her and felt its fire burn down her throat, jolting life back into her veins.

'Thank you,' she whispered.

Alex crouched down on his haunches so that she did not have to look up at him. His eyes commanded her attention and he took one of her hands and pressed it tightly to reinforce the command.

'Now listen to me. I have to leave you and take control up there so that the situation doesn't get out of hand. Do you understand?'

'Yes. I'm all right,' she forced out jerkily.

'No, you're in shock, but hold on tight. I'll get you through this. Just sit here and don't move. I'll be back as soon as I can.'

She nodded and closed her eyes, unable to muster the strength to do anything but obey him. She heard the fuss and bustle as Fiona was brought down to the saloon, sobbing hysterically. She heard Jan Lister try to quieten her with soothing words. It all washed over Kate like some horrible nightmare.

'She doesn't care! Scott was divorcing her. Why the hell should I consider her? The cunning bitch has already feathered her nest with Alex Dalton . . .'

The ugly words were cut off with a hard slap.

'Shut up, Fiona!' Bob Chardway's voice had an unaccustomed ring of authority.

Kate looked across at them. She felt oddly detached, as if she was watching them from a great distance.

Fiona's mouth dropped open as she gasped at her husband. 'You hit me!'

'Yes, and I'll hit you again if you don't keep

your lip buttoned,' Bob retorted sharply. 'We've
got enough trouble on our hands. Questions are
going to be asked and you're going to be very
discreet, Fiona, because Scott wouldn't have been
out there but for you.'

She burst into noisy sobs again. 'Oh God!
Don't say that, Bob. Don't say that.'

Kate watched the others trying to console
Fiona, patting her, fetching her a drink, tucking a
blanket around her. They were all acting as if
Fiona was the widow. No one looked at Kate.
They seemed to be pretending that she did not
exist. And she did not exist for them any more.
She had only existed as an appendage of Scott.

She was alone, bobbing aimlessly on a wave of
intense desolation. Then she was not alone. Alex
Dalton was there and he was looking at her. He
saw her. He seemed to be looking straight into
her soul. It was an eerie sensation, as if they were
in a special capsule of time, just the two of them.
He leaned over and took the glass of brandy from
her hand. She had forgotten it was there. Then
he was pulling her to her feet.

'Come on. I'm putting you to bed. The police-
launch is on its way and I won't have you sitting
through an inquiry. There are more than enough
witnesses.'

'No . . . should stay . . .' she began in fluttery
protest, but the blood was draining from her face,
causing her to lose balance.

He caught her up and cradled her against his
broad chest. With a swift economy of movement
he carried her into the same stateroom they had
occupied earlier, flicked aside the velvet bedspread, carefully lowered her on to the pillow,

then tucked the bedspread around her.

'Trust me,' he said gently. 'There's no point in your being out there. Just rest. I'll send Jan Lister in to sit with you in case you need anything. As soon as I get rid of the police I'll be back, and then we can talk.'

CHAPTER FOUR

KATE watched him go, too listless to really care about anything. He was right. There was no point in her staying out there. She was only an embarrassment to the others, an unwanted presence. She wondered what Alex wanted to talk to her about. Her life was in a mess, but she didn't want to talk about that. She didn't want to talk at all.

She thought about Scott. His pointless death seemed a savage reflection of their whole pointless marriage, five years whose only legacy was a residue of ugliness, a messy ending to a messy partnership. Non-partnership. Scott had only ever considered himself.

She could not simply walk away tomorrow. A clean break was now impossible. Scott's death trapped her into the role of his widow, burdening her with the responsibility of tying up all the strings he had played with, and those strings were bound to contain unpleasant snags. Her husband had never chosen to be straightforward about anything.

A great weariness of body and soul had settled on her, anaesthetising all emotion. She lay there like a limp doll in a drifting vacuum.

Jan Lister came in, carrying Kate's handbag. 'Thought you might need it if you wanted to freshen up. Alex said there's an en-suite bathroom . . .' She glanced around and nodded to a door. 'Must be through there.'

'Thanks,' Kate mumbled, wishing that Alex had not sent Jan to keep her company. She did not want to talk and Jan was a compulsive talker.

She sat on the edge of the bed and looked at Kate with eyes which were more curious than sympathetic. 'You really are shaken up, aren't you?'

Kate sighed and turned her head restlessly on the pillow. 'I'm all right.'

'Well, anyhow, Alex seems intent on looking after you. Rather a masterful type, I must say. He was laying down the law out there as I came in.'

Kate made no comment but Jan was not discouraged. She kept prattling on.

'Poor old Scott! God! What a horrible accident! I've never been so shocked in all my life. I just hope it teaches Fiona a lesson. She's too much, isn't she? Flaunting herself like that today. She didn't get any change out of Alex though. Was it true about you and Scott getting a divorce?'

'Yes,' Kate muttered irritably.

'Well, I don't blame you for latching on to Alex. Scott was a pig to you anyway. You should have heard the snide cracks he made about you when you were down here with Alex.'

Kate was jolted out of her dull passivity. Of course. That was why the others had stood back and left her alone. It wasn't just Fiona. They all thought ... 'Jan, you're wrong!' she cried urgently. 'Nothing happened down here this morning. Alex and I just talked, that's all. He's simply being kind to me.'

'Kind?' Jan shook her head mockingly. 'My dear Kate, men like Alex Dalton aren't kind for nothing. Oh, I believe you if you say nothing happened this morning, but I bet that was your decision, not his. And he's certainly staking his claim now. If you ask me . . .'

Kate was not asking anything and she did not listen to any more. Her mind was suddenly feverish with thoughts. Alex would have made love to her. He had admitted it quite cynically. It had all been a game to him. Was his kindness a new game? Trust me, he had said, but she could not trust a man. Scott had never been straight and Alex Dalton was even more devious than Scott. He was out there now, handling everything to spare her unpleasantness, but there would be a price to be paid for his kindness. There was always a price to be paid for anything. Scott had taught her that.

Men made her sick. Everything they handed out was simply a line to get a woman into bed. Alex Dalton was not a grabber. He was a far more subtle man than that. A dangerous man. And she was lying here in his bed. Where he had placed her.

Kate flung aside the bedspread, swung her feet to the floor and sat up. A wave of dizziness struck her again and bile surged up her throat, spreading its sourness into her mouth before she could swallow it back down. Her weakness was frustrating but she fought it, forcing herself to stand.

'What are you getting up for?' Jan fluttered with concern. 'You look ghastly.'

'I'm going to have a wash. Would you pass me my handbag please, Jan?'

'Here you are. Well, give me a call if you need me.'

By supporting herself against the vanity cupboard Kate could manage. She grimaced at her reflection in the mirror. Her hair was in disarray and mascara was smudged around her eyes. A brisk scrub with soap and water removed the make-up but revealed the putty greyness of her skin. The light sprinkling of freckles across her cheeks and nose stood out sharply. Shock had stripped her of any attractiveness but Kate did not bother re-applying make-up. There was no compulsion now to make herself look attractive.

She took a hair brush from her handbag and tried to subdue the unruly mass of red-gold waves, wishing fiercely that she had brought some hairpins. Then in search of some toothpaste to take the sick taste out of her mouth, Kate opened a drawer of the vanity.

A comprehensive array of female necessities was neatly set out; a complete range of make-up, cleansing cream, tissues, hairpins, a shower-cap, even a brush and comb. She stared at them. Alex Dalton was a very thoughtful man. She cynically wondered how many women had shared his bed and subsequently availed themselves of these cosmetics. After a moment's hesitation she took some hairpins and folded her hair into a conservative pleat.

Another drawer yielded a variety of soaps and toothpastes and several toothbrushes still wrapped in cellophane. Obviously overnight guests were also catered for. Deciding that Alex Dalton could afford to have one toothbrush wasted, Kate gave her mouth a more wholesome taste. Feeling considerably fresher and more composed, she made her way back to the stateroom.

Jan started guiltily from the porthole window. Kate sucked in a deep breath as nausea hit her again.

'I suppose they're searching for . . . for Scott's body,' she said, forcing herself to remain calm.

'Yes,' Jan muttered, embarrassed at having been caught indulging her morbid curiosity.

'I'm joining the others.'

'Alex won't like it.'

'Alex Dalton is not my keeper,' Kate retorted and marched over to the door.

Alex was the only person absent from the saloon. Everyone's head turned towards her, expressions varying from surprise to resentment.

'Well, the frail little widow makes her entrance,' Fiona jeered, 'very conveniently waiting until the police have gone.'

'Shut up, Fiona,' Bob clipped out warningly.

'The heavy protector's not here,' she snapped back at him. 'I'll say what I like.'

There was a collective hiss, a perceptible stiffening. Alex Dalton stood at the head of the stairs. His casual clothes and easy-going manner had been replaced by tailored slacks, a lightweight jacket, and an air of ruthless authority. His gaze sliced around the company. Kate was the last to come within his line of vision. She was still near the stateroom door. He frowned and headed straight for her, ignoring everyone else.

'Why couldn't you do as I asked?' he chided gently, scanning her pale face. 'You don't look well enough to be on your feet and there's nothing for you to do. Come, I'll take you back.'

His arm began sliding around her shoulders and Kate stiffened, fiercely resenting the intimacy he was projecting. She was acutely aware of the wave of antagonism which rippled towards them out of the watching silence. The others were coupling her with Alex and he was reinforcing that coupling. She took a sharp step away from him, asserting her independence.

'I'm well enough, thank you. You've been very kind, Alex, but I don't need to be treated as an invalid. I'll cope.'

Fiona gave a derisive laugh which ended abruptly in a gasp. Her glare at her husband spoke eloquently of silent intervention. Bob Chardway's face was grim with disgust, but whether it was disgust at himself or his wife or the whole day's events, it was impossible to tell.

Alex's scathing gaze took them all in before returning to Kate. 'Did no one offer you comfort, a chair, a drink, a friendly word?'

She flushed, all too aware that none of Scott's friends cared a fig for her, but embarrassed by Alex's blunt emphasis of the fact.

'Kate has only just come out, Alex,' Terry Jessell jumped in, anxious to exonerate himself.

Alex made no acknowledgment that Terry had even spoken. He took Kate's elbow and steered her to an armchair. She sat down with a sinking feeling of helplessness, wondering how she was going to extricate herself from this situation. Alex Dalton was deliberately drawing a line, separating her from the others and placing himself squarely at her side.

A deckhand came clattering down the stairs and Alex turned towards him. 'Everything in order?'

'Yessir. About to go.'

There was a general sigh of relief and Alex waited a moment before addressing all of them. 'We will be moving slowly out of the area so as not to interfere with the search which is proceeding. You can expect to be back at the jetty in half an hour. The dinghy will make two trips. The Chardways and Listers will be taken ashore first. Terry, you and your wife will wait and accompany Kate and myself.' He waved towards the deckhand. 'Darrell, here, will serve drinks to anyone who wishes to have one. Tea and coffee will be available in a few minutes.'

Having delivered what were in effect, unarguable orders, Alex drew a chair close to Kate's and sat down, his concentration solely on her. Kate concentrated on her hands, evading his searching gaze.

'Common sense should come before pride, Mary Kathleen,' he said softly.

She flicked a wary look at him. 'I think it's more sensible of me to be out here. I ought to know what's happening.'

'Apart from what you heard me say a moment ago, I've arranged that the police not visit you until tomorrow morning, and Terry Jessell has undertaken to explain the circumstances of Scott's death to his family. That frees you of any worries for tonight.'

Free for what purpose, Kate thought suspiciously. On the surface it sounded very considerate, but he had also linked her name to his for the trip in the dinghy, and she did not want to be linked to him in any way whatsoever.

'That was thoughtful of you, Alex, but it's my duty to go and see Scott's parents,' she said tightly.

'You don't owe Scott anything.'

'But his parents . . .'

'Will only burden you with guilt, expecting you to share their grief.'

'You assume too much, Alex.'

'Did you want to grieve with them?'

'It's not a matter of wanting to grieve.'

'Then forget it. No one'll thank you for the stiff upper lip and you've had enough to put up with. Don't turn Scott's death into a hypocritical farce. You were finished with him. Now you're permanently finished with him.'

A door at the rear of the saloon opened to admit a trolley wheeled by a man in a chef's uniform. Alex stood up to direct the serving of refreshments and Kate was relieved to be free of his company. His callous reading of the situation had upset her, unreasonably so since it was brutally honest. She would not grieve for Scott. The Scott who had died today had lost all rights to her love and respect.

She had told Alex Dalton too much this morning. She did not want him or any man involving himself in her life. His self-appointed role of protector had to be squashed. She accepted the cup of tea he handed her, but when he resumed his seat she turned to him with a coolly polite face.

'I'm very grateful for the kindness and consideration you've shown me this afternoon, but there's no need to trouble yourself any further on my account, I can manage alone from now on.'

Keen blue eyes probed her guarded expression. One eyebrow rose mockingly. 'A polite dismissal, Mary Kathleen?'

Embarrassment lent a faint colour to her cheeks. 'The cruise is almost over,' she replied with pointed emphasis.

'But it's not ending as it started. The circumstances are vastly different.'

'My circumstances, not yours, Alex. You were our host for the day. That's all.'

'And as your host I'll see you safely home,' he said smoothly.

'I can drive myself and I prefer to be alone,' she insisted with even more emphasis.

'I don't intend to let you go alone.'

His tone of voice irritated her, scraping as it did over the raw wounds of Scott's bullying. 'I'll do as I please,' she stated coldly and ignored him, drinking her tea in small sips.

Jan Lister took the opportunity to break into their conversation. 'Kate, I'll drop by tomorrow. Dennis and I are going up on deck ready to leave so I'll say goodbye now. Thanks for your hospitality, Alex.'

Dennis came forward and offered his hand to Alex. 'Good of you to handle everything so well,' he muttered and nodded awkwardly to Kate before almost pulling Jan away and hurrying her up the stairs.

Fiona Chardway stood and followed them with a haughty toss of the head. Bob threw an exasperated look after her then strolled over, head bent and hands thrust in his pockets.

'Uh, Kate. You can contact me when you feel up to it. I've got Scott's will and other papers of his in safe keeping. Just give me a tinkle, eh? We'll get it sorted out.'

'Thanks, Bob,' she said stiffly, his ill-at-ease

manner rubbing off on her.

'Uh ... better go.' He thrust out one hand. 'G'bye, Alex.'

'I'll see you off.'

'No need,' Bob hastily assured him, lifting his proffered hand in protest. 'We'll be all right. Stay with Kate.' He backed away as he spoke, waved a farewell salute to the Jessells, then jogged up the stairs.

Terry rose from his chair, lifting Wendy up by the elbow as he stood. 'We'll see them off and wait up on deck for the dinghy to return. Okay?'

'Please yourself,' Alex nodded carelessly.

Their readiness to leave, their almost indecent haste, did not surprise Kate one bit. Scott's friends were not people who were prepared to get involved with anything unpleasant. They were only too relieved to let Alex look after her. 'Rats,' she breathed in a bitter comment.

Alex caught the word and amusement twitched at his lips. 'The ship is not sinking.'

She flashed a derisive look at him. 'The ship that carried me has sunk. Scott's dead and I'm nothing to any one of them. Not that I care. What did you say to them?'

'You heard me.'

'I mean before the police got here.'

He shrugged. 'Just a few words to restore order.'

'Like what?'

He waved a dismissive hand. 'I simply told them to stick to the bare facts and persuaded them that any straying off that course was ... not wise. I added something to the effect that you were to be spoken of only in terms of the highest respect.'

'Oh God!' she sighed wearily. 'That really sealed it. You know what they think.'

'They're not wrong.'

His soft assertion brought a swift wave of indignation. 'You know perfectly well they're wrong!'

'The minor misconception that we've been physically intimate is irrelevant,' he drawled. 'I've made no secret of my interest in you and you accepted my friendship, Mary Kathleen.'

'Will you stop calling me that! My name is Kate! Kate, do you hear?' she cried in agitated protest. He gave her full name too personal a flavour. She could feel him moving in on her and all her instincts told her he was too dangerous a man to let close.

'Very well. Kate . . . if you insist.'

'And I didn't accept your friendship,' she continued defensively. 'At least, only for today. Just to get Scott off my back.' She swallowed hard as she recalled how hideously Scott had been removed from her back.

'Today isn't over. You need me, Kate.'

'I don't!' she snapped, her eyes fiercely rejecting him. 'I don't need you or anyone. I'll stand on my own two feet.' She sprang up to emphasise the point. An attack of dizziness made her sway and she clutched at her head in an attempt to steady it.

'You're not strong enough at the moment to do anything alone.' He rose and gathered her into his arms, ignoring the weak flutter of her hands and the frantic appeal of her eyes. 'Relax. Don't fight me. I'm simply supporting you. You looked as if you were about to faint.'

'Let me go! I'm all right,' she panted, pushing against his formidable strength. His embrace was too disturbing whatever his motive. Power seemed to emanate from him and Kate panicked as she felt its attraction. The temptation to lean on him had to be resisted. If she was ever to learn independence she had to start asserting her own will now.

'No, you're not all right,' he refuted her gently. One large hand captured both of hers and held them still while his other arm kept her pinned against him. His eyes probed the feverish anxiety in hers. 'Why are you frightened of me?'

'I'm not. I'm not,' she denied too quickly, then tried desperately to calm her galloping pulse. 'I just want you to let me go. I don't like being touched.'

His eyes narrowed on the clear signs of tension. 'It seems your husband was more stupid than I gave him credit for,' he muttered and lowered her back into the chair she had vacated. He dropped back into his own chair and drummed his fingers on the armrest, his expression darkly brooding.

Kate was grateful for the respite from his attention. She enclosed herself in a cocoon of silence, blocking him out and thinking ahead to the tasks in front of her.

'I'll drive you home.'

She glanced at him, vexed by his persistence.

He waved his hand in a pre-emptive dismissal of any protest. 'Don't argue. Clearly you're not well enough to handle a car through the city traffic.'

Kate had to admit it was only common sense to

accept his offer. 'Thank you,' she dragged out reluctantly.

He smiled acknowledgement of her grudging surrender but said no more. It was not long before one of the crew informed them that the dinghy was returning for its second trip. Kate's legs felt like jelly as she walked upstairs. She did not resit Alex's supporting hand on her elbow. The short trip to the jetty was accomplished under a veneer of social ease since Terry thought it expedient to engage Alex in conversation. The climb up the sandstone steps seemed endless to Kate. Alex halted her as they drew level to a door into his garage.

'I'll see you in the morning, Terry,' he said by way of farewell to the Jessells.

'Right, Alex,' Terry nodded, his expression eloquent of relief. 'I'll take Wendy home and then visit the Andrews. Anything else I can do for you, Kate, just let me know,' he added, but the perfunctory comment was directed more at Alex than her.

'Thanks, Terry.' At least she did not have to face the Andrews today. For that she was grateful.

Wendy plucked at his elbow and Terry took the hint. Kate watched them go out the gateway as Alex handed keys to the lad who had tied up the dinghy and trailed up the steps after them.

'Just follow me. I won't be driving fast,' Alex instructed him.

Kate resisted as he tried to lead her into the garage. 'My car's out there.'

'Kevin will drive it. We'll go in mine and I can bring him back,' Alex explained reasonably.

It was a sleek, green Lamborghini. Kate

huddled into the cold, leather passenger seat, not in any mood to appreciate the luxury of the car. Alex drove with smooth expertise. The late Sunday afternoon traffic was heavy. Everyone going home, Kate thought dully, just as she was going home. Only her house had never been a home. A home was where children were raised in the security of love. She would sell her house, remove herself from its emptiness.

'I don't intend to let you go, Kate.'

The calmly stated words forced her attention on to the man in the driver's seat. 'What's that supposed to mean?'

He threw her a measuring look before switching his gaze back to the road. 'It means I like you, I want you, and now that Scott's dead, I intend to have you.'

Kate's breath caught in her throat. She expelled it slowly as she gathered her shocked wits together. A thousand resentments against male domination lent acid to her tongue. 'There is a little matter of my consent. Or were you considering rape?'

His soft chuckle was accompanied by an odd look of triumph. 'Yes. You'll do. In fact I'm liking you better all the time. Rape doesn't figure in my plans and gaining your consent is no little matter, but it shall be done.'

She stared out the side-window, disdaining to reply to such arrogance. For all his wealth and influence, Alex Dalton could not get near her unless she allowed him to. For the first time in five years she was in sole control of her life and she would do exactly what she wanted to do, not what some man told her.

Having calmed herself with this self-assurance, Kate nevertheless felt a surge of relief when the car pulled up outside her house. She quickly alighted, not waiting for Alex to open the passenger-door. Sheer willpower walked her legs across the lawn to where Kevin was parking Scott's station-wagon. He looked up, handed her the keys and mumbled some answer to her thanks. Alex was waiting for her on the front porch. He held out Scott's wallet.

'I didn't think you'd want his clothes.'

'No . . . thank you. And thank you for bringing me home. Goodbye, Alex,' she added firmly, repelling the warmth of his gaze with ice-blue eyes.

'Not goodbye, Kate,' he said with quiet confidence. 'We can be of use to each other. Think about it.' He started walking down the path.

'The answer is no. You have nothing that could tempt me, Alex,' she declared coldly.

He glanced back, the strong face lined with deep cynicism. 'I doubt that, Mary Kathleen.'

She bit back the words which soured her tongue and turned away, fumbling with the keys before inserting the right one in the front door. She opened it and stepped inside, closing the door decisively against the whole rotten world, including Alex Dalton.

CHAPTER FIVE

IT was stupid to give way now. The worst was over. Kate hugged herself tightly and blinked back the tears. The morning so far had been more harrowing than she could have imagined with reporters on her doorstep, the visit from the police and the subsequent trip to the morgue.

She shivered. It had been like a horrible nightmare and the memory was too sharp to dismiss. The antiseptic smell was still in her nostrils. The image of a white-sheathed bundle which was not a body was imprinted on her brain. Scott's face had been unmarked, just as they had assured her, but it had been so terribly lifeless. She rubbed at her eyes, wishing she could erase the picture. It was over, she told herself sternly, and at least she had got through it without leaning on anyone.

Her employer had given her two weeks' compassionate leave and Kate was satisfied that she had made an organised start to the day. Scott's parents were to visit her this afternoon at the same time as an agent from a funeral home. She had telephoned Scott's office, intent on coming to some arrangement with Terry about winding up the partnership. Terry had been absent but she had left a message with the office girl for him to call on her as soon as it was convenient. Bob Chardway still had to be contacted. She was lifting the telephone when the doorbell rang. Kate hesitated, reluctant to answer any more summons this morning. Then with a resigned sigh she put down the telephone.

Jan Lister greeted her with a sympathetic smile and a supermarket bag. 'Thought I'd drop by with some provisions to pamper you with. How are you, Kate?'

'Managing. Thanks, Jan. It's very kind of you.'

'Lead me into the kitchen and let's have a cup of coffee.' She did not wait to be led. 'Truth of the matter is, I felt a bit guilty about leaving you yesterday and wanted to see if you were all right. You don't look too good.'

'It's been a rather nerve-racking morning.' Kate switched on the percolator, resigned to having company.

Jan hitched herself on to a kitchen stool and lifted a cake out of the bag. 'You need to build up your energy. Cut yourself a big slice of this and get it down you. I would've stayed yesterday but Dennis insisted we go and Alex made it pretty clear that he was taking you over.'

'Taking me over?' Kate echoed sharply. She flicked an irritable look at Jan. 'Alex Dalton just happened to be our host. I do not expect to have anything further to do with him.'

Jan eyed her sceptically. 'Kate, I don't go along with Fiona's reading of the situation, but Alex certainly showed more than a passing interest in you, and if you ask me, you'd be an absolute idiot to pass him up.'

'What do you suggest? That I become mistress number fifty-seven?' she retorted bitterly. 'That's a bit much, don't you think, when Scott's lying dead in a morgue?'

Jan sighed and made a discomforted gesture. 'Well, you did admit yesterday that your marriage was over anyway. I'm sorry Scott's dead but let's face it, you weren't happy with him. How could you be when . . . well, you must have at least known about Fiona. They both made it pretty obvious.'

Kate poured out the coffee, cut pieces of cake and gestured to Jan to help herself to anything she wanted. Having settled herself on another stool she propped her head in her hands and looked wearily at her visitor. 'I don't want to think about that.'

Jan shrugged and heaped sugar into her coffee. 'You've got to think of the future though. What are you going to do, Kate?'

'I don't know. Get the funeral over. I'll sell this house. I'll work it all out eventually, I suppose,' she said dispiritedly.

'Alex Dalton could ease you over the rough spots.'

'No, thanks. It'll be a long time before I let another man into my life.'

'It's not much fun being on your own.' She made an exasperated sound. 'Look! You've got one of the richest bachelors in Sydney interested in you. Why don't you see where it can lead? Use your head, Kate. You know what I thought when we were having lunch yesterday? That it would serve Scott right if you walked off with Alex Dalton. Scott wasn't doing anything to keep you and why shouldn't you enjoy the kind of life Alex could offer? You haven't any kids to hold you back.'

'No, I haven't any kids. Do you think Alex

Dalton is interested in marriage and babies?' she asked derisively.

'You never know. . . .'

Kate gave a brittle laugh.

'You seemed to be getting on well with him.'

'Did I? To tell you the truth he frightens me.'

'Why? What's there to be frightened of?'

'I don't know. It's like he's in control and I'm not. I let Scott take too much from me and I have to find myself again. I don't want to be a wishy-washy person any more, bending to another's will. I have to learn to be me.'

Jan looked at her as if she thought Kate was floundering in stupidity. With an air of straightening her out she said slowly, 'Let's suppose Alex Dalton wants a relationship with you. There's no reason why you can't control it. You don't have to take anything from him you don't want.'

Kate gave a wry smile. 'Anyone trying to control Alex Dalton would get trampled underfoot, and I'm trying to pick myself up off the ground as it is.'

'All the same, Kate, there's no harm in giving it a try. Think of all that lovely wealth.'

Kate did not pursue the subject. Jan Lister would never understand her point of view. All Scott's friends had one thing in common, their preoccupation with money, how to get it and how to spend it to impress others. Jan's visit had obviously been prompted by curiosity about Alex Dalton. When her efforts to pursue the subject fell on barren ground she took her leave, making a belated enquiry about Scott's funeral as Kate accompanied her to the door.

After she had gone Kate unpacked the grocery parcel. Its contents amused her; frozen pizza, frozen potato chips, frozen quiche lorraine, more cake and sweet biscuits. It was not surprising that Jan had a weight problem if this was her choice of diet. Still, there had been kindness behind the thought and Kate's pantry was virtually empty. She had spent almost all of last week's house-keeping money on Scott's dinner-party and she was grateful to have some easy-to-prepare food in the house.

When the doorbell rang again she glanced quickly at the clock. It confirmed that there was an hour to go before the Andrews' visit. Hoping the caller might be Terry Jessell she hurried to the door.

'So you are home! I wondered if you would be,' Fiona Chardway said waspishly. 'You don't have to hide behind the door. I'm not going to bite.'

'What do you want, Fiona?' Kate asked coldly, not at all disposed to be civil to Scott's former mistress.

Suddenly there was a flicker of fear in her eyes, a wheedle of appeasement in her voice. 'Look, Kate, I know you don't have any time for me and I wouldn't have bothered you if I wasn't worried out of my mind. Let me come in and talk to you. It's terribly urgent and private.'

Kate could not imagine anything urgent which Fiona might need to communicate but she led her into the lounge. Fiona sat down and took her time lighting a cigarette, her eyes evading any direct line to Kate until she had puffed nervously at it several times.

'I might as well come straight out with it,' she began defiantly. 'I wrote Scott some letters. I don't know if he destroyed them. I've been to his office and they're not there. If Bob saw them . . . I expect you'll ask him to go through Scott's papers. Would you . . . check that there's nothing incriminating among them beforehand? When all's said and done he is my husband.'

'And Scott was my husband. Did you ever consider that, Fiona?' Kate demanded bitterly, remembering all too well the humiliations of Scott's infidelities.

'Oh, don't come the prissy, wronged woman with me,' Fiona scoffed irritably. 'Scott wouldn't have been straying if he'd been satisfied at home. And what do you care now? You've got Alex Dalton. The letters can't hurt you but they can hurt me. It's not that I care much for Bob but I've got two kids and he's a good provider even if he is an occasional drunk.'

Suddenly the thought of using Bob Chardway as her solicitor was repugnant to Kate. 'You needn't worry, Fiona. Bob'll never see the letters if they still exist. I'll go to another solicitor.'

'Oh, don't be ridiculous!' Fiona spat back, her resentment at having to ask a favour overcoming all discretion. 'Bob knows all Scott's business. All I'm asking you to do . . .'

'That's enough!' Kate stood up. 'You're not welcome in this house any more.'

Fiona rose with a haughty look of disdain. 'I suppose Alex Dalton's got you all fixed up with a fancy solicitor. Not wasting any time, is he?'

'If I hear you linking Alex Dalton with me

again I'll send those letters to your husband. Now get out!'

Fiona sniffed as she passed by but she went without further argument. Kate closed the door after her with such a feeling of utter revulsion that she felt ill. Knowing that she could only anticipate a difficult afternoon with Harry and Sheila Andrews she went upstairs and lay down in an attempt to settle her jangling nerves.

As it turned out, the undertaker arrived soon after Scott's parents and Kate was spared from having to mouth too many hypocritical platitudes. Having just suffered Fiona's visit, she found it extremely distasteful to commiserate with Sheila Andrews as she tearfully enumerated Scott's virtues. Funeral arrangements were discussed and agreed upon. The morbid details upset Scott's mother even further and Kate tactfully suggested to her father-in-law that it might be best to cut the visit short.

Kate privately blessed the lucky chance which brought Terry Jessell to her doorstep just as she was ushering them out. It gave her a ready excuse to make the onerous leave-taking brief.

'You look as if you could do with a drink,' Terry remarked as she joined him in the lounge.

'You're right,' she said feelingly.

'Sit down and relax. I'll pour you one.'

'Thanks, Terry. And thanks for breaking the news to Harry and Sheila yesterday. It was good of you.'

'A hell of a thing to have happened! Poor old Scott!' He shook his head and busied himself behind the bar.

Kate closed her eyes out of sheer weariness of

spirit. There were so many things she had to ask Terry and it took all her energy to concentrate her mind. She heard him approach and forced her lids open again. He handed her a whisky and took the seat opposite her.

'Fact is, Kate, that bastard . . . uh . . . well . . . Scott and I were kind of counting on Alex Dalton to give us the lift we needed, and he backed off this morning. No deal.'

He was uneasy, not quite meeting her eyes. Kate said nothing but a heavy cynicism settled on her heart.

'You must have known we were skating on pretty thin ice. There's nothing for you out of the business, Kate. We were barely making ends meet with a big overdraft. The books will show you that. I suppose you'll be getting an accountant in to do an audit.'

An accountant. She would need an accountant as well as a solicitor, Kate thought despondently. 'I expected you'd be able to help me with Scott's business affairs, Terry.'

He backed off so fast it was sickening. His chin jerked up and his hands lifted in protest. 'Not me, Kate. It'd be unethical with the partnership and all. You get someone in to represent your interests. Besides, I know nothing of Scott's personal stuff. Don't even know if he had insurance.'

'Neither do I,' Kate sighed.

'Well, you'd better go through his personal papers, or take them to Bob. He'll help you. That's what solicitors are for. It'd be wrong for me to interfere, you know. I've got to protect my own interests.' He flushed, conscious of how tactless that had sounded. 'You understand what I mean, Kate,' he added hurriedly.

'Yes, I understand. Thank you for being so direct, Terry. It's best that I know I can't rely on you for anything.'

'I say, that's a bit strong, Kate,' he protested in a fluster.

'I'm sorry. Were you going to suggest being a pall-bearer at Scott's funeral?' she said with a touch of acid.

'Yes, of course,' he said quickly. 'I'd be honoured.'

'You're easily honoured.' Kate put her glass down and pointedly stood up. 'Well, Terry, thank you for calling on me. I presume you'll give full co-operation to my accountant.'

He down his whisky and rose with an eagerness which said more clearly than words how glad he was to be rid of any responsibility. 'I dare say Alex Dalton can put you on to a good man.'

Kate gave him a scathing look. 'You, too.'

'What do you mean?'

'Nothing. Think what you like. I don't care what any of you think. Goodbye, Terry. The funeral will be on Thursday if you can bring yourself to attend.'

'Now, Kate . . .'

'Oh, for God's sake, go.'

'You're upset.'

'Yes, I'm upset. Oddly enough. My husband died yesterday. This morning I had to identify his body. All in all it's been quite a day. Now please go and leave me alone.'

He was dithering, thrown off-balance because Kate had denied him a polite retreat. She strode impatiently to the front door and flung it open. He followed hesitantly, agitation written all over his face.

'Listen, Kate, don't get me wrong . . .'

'I haven't got you wrong, Terry. Goodbye.'

'I'll be there on Thursday, Kate. You can count on me,' he assured her effusively as he sidled out the door.

'Of course, Terry. I'm sure you'll see Scott off in style,' she said grimly and shut the door in his face.

Rage burned through every vein in her body. Every cheap deception in her marriage scorched through her mind, all the empty years which had been wasted with people like Terry Jessell, Fiona Chardway, Jan Lister, and most of all, Scott himself. Never again, Kate promised herself savagely. She had been young, innocent, impressionable, lost in a jungle she could not relate to, but her eyes were wide open now and she would walk down her own path in the future, choosing each step with the wisdom of bitter experience.

Still seething with anger but armed with determination Kate went to Scott's desk and emptied all the drawers on to the dining-room table. She fetched an empty carton from the garage and started sifting through the papers Scott had left. The carton was full when she finished. Only a small, neat pile remained on the table and it contributed more to the hollowness of Kate's stomach than any lack of food. Unpaid bills, notes of loans, insurance policies which had lapsed, a heavy mortgage on the house, bankbooks which contained far too little to balance the debts. They added up to financial disaster.

She needed an accountant all right, Kate thought despairingly as she took a break and ate some of the quiche lorraine which Jan had brought. The pastry seemed to stick in her throat but a cup of coffee helped wash it down. The doorbell rang again. Kate decided to ignore it. For ten minutes she held out against the insistent summons, then with a sigh of exasperation she answered it.

Alex Dalton stood there. Kate sucked in a quick breath, trying to stem the rush of emotion. It was a vain attempt. She exploded. 'You! You're all I need to make my day complete!'

'Nice to know I'm needed,' he replied blandly and stepped inside before she had wits enough to stop him.

'I don't need you!' she insisted vehemently.

'You just said you did.'

Tears of frustration sprang to her eyes and she slammed the door in helpless temper. 'I didn't mean it, damn you!' She leaned against the door, biting her lips as she swallowed back the hysteria which rose in her throat. Her eyes accused him of adding to her inner misery.

'Rough day,' he murmured and stepped towards her.

'Don't you touch me!' she cried wildly. 'I told you goodbye. I don't want you here. I don't want anyone. You're all . . . all . . . contemptible.'

'A very rough day,' he nodded.

The sympathy in his voice and the soft gleam of caring in his eyes wilted her aggression. She looked at him with tired pain. 'What do you want, Alex?'

'I want you, Mary Kathleen. I've thought of nothing else all day. You can walk away from all your problems right now. I'll take care of everything. All you have to do is say yes.'

CHAPTER SIX

SHE stared at him unseeingly, her mind turning over the temptation he offered. It would be wonderful to forget everything and just walk away, to unburden herself of all responsibility, have no worries at all. There was no one to stop her, no one to care what she did. She could have a pleasant life of ease all for the price of pleasing Alex. Pleasing Alex . . . in bed. The rosy bubble burst and harsh bitter laughter erupted from her throat.

'Oh God!' she gasped, her eyes mocking him viciously. 'That's what they all think. One by one they've come today, dropping your name as the answer to all my problems. The answer!' she repeated derisively. 'Is that how you see yourself, Alex?'

He shrugged, completely unperturbed by her reaction. 'It was worth a try. You looked very vulnerable. However, I see you've recovered your defences so I'll make do with your company and conversation. What else has happened today?' He turned and strolled casually into the dining-room which was the only lighted room in the house and obviously where she had been sitting. 'I'm glad you've been sensible enough to eat.'

Kate followed him, burning with resentment. She snatched up her plate and mug and took them to the kitchen, returning to find Alex leafing through the pile of papers.

'Have you got a good accountant?' he asked matter-of-factly.

'No. Would you like to recommend one?' she retorted sarcastically.

'Peterson. Carl Peterson. I have his number here.' He fished out his wallet and extracted a business-card. 'Very efficient man. Knows how to juggle everything to your best interests.'

'How clever of him! Is your solicitor a wizard too?'

'Naturally. I always try to employ the best men available.' He extracted another card and dropped them both on the table. One eyebrow rose quizzically. 'Anything else I can help you with?'

'I didn't ask for your help. I was under the impression I had just rejected all you had to offer.'

He grinned, his eyes dancing wickedly at her. 'I don't mind losing the first round. Nor the second. It's time spent in learning the qualities of my opponent. And I am delighted with your qualities, Mary Kathleen.'

'Don't call me that!' she snapped, tension rising in her as he drew out a chair and sat down, making himself completely at home. The man was impossible to handle, a law unto himself.

He smiled at her. 'Don't stand there all tensed like a cobra about to strike. Tonight I'll be your friend. Sit down and relax. Pour out all your troubles.'

Her nerves were stretched to breaking-point. Alex Dalton's continued presence was the last thing she needed for relaxation. 'I don't want to fight with you, Alex. I don't want to be in the same ring with you. Please go,' she said stiffly.

'Why? What do you plan to do? Grieve for the selfish bastard you married? Lick your wounds so constantly that you can't taste anything else? What good will that do? Better to talk with me.'

He was not going to budge. He sat there as immovable as the Rock of Gibraltar. With a defeated sigh Kate dropped into a chair and eyed him warily. 'What do you want with me? Can't you see I'm not interested in your kind of game?'

'I don't have a game in mind, Mary Kathleen. More like a contract,' he replied with a touch of whimsy, a faint smile curving his lips. 'Yes, a contract,' he repeated, watching her with sharp interest. 'What would you say to a contract of marriage? I don't think you could classify that as a game.'

Kate stared at him disbelievingly for a long moment, then propped her elbows on the table and covered her face with her hands. 'I'm not playing,' she muttered wearily.

'Neither am I.'

She dragged her hands down a little and searched his expression for any trace of mockery or amusement. Her heart gave a funny little lurch when she realised there was none. 'You're seriously proposing marriage to me?' she asked, still not quite believing him.

'I think we could serve each other well,' he replied carelessly.

'What's that supposed to mean?'

His eyes were watchful, intensely concentrated on her, even though his manner remained relaxed. His hand moved in an airy gesture of invitation. 'Tell me what you want for the rest of your life.'

She let out her breath in an exasperated sigh. 'Oh, this is crazy!'

'Tell me,' he insisted quietly.

'Do you imagine you can give me everything I want?'

He nodded with all the confidence of a man who was used to success. 'Materially, yes. No question about it. You would never be insecure financially again. That's one problem you could discard immediately.'

'Working on the principle that money buys everything,' she mocked.

'Not at all. It buys a certain amount of comfort and freedom. It doesn't buy children.'

She knew as he spoke those last words that he had perceived her own dearest wish. Her mind switched back to the dinner-party when he had questioned her so pointedly on the subject. Somehow he had picked up her frustration and now he was using it, calmly, knowingly, and to devastating effect. She glanced down at her rings, symbols of promises which had been broken over and over again. All the bleak barrenness of her marriage was shadowed in her eyes as she looked back at him.

'Do you really want children?'

He spread his hands as if he had nothing to hide. 'Why else would I propose marriage? What possible advantage is it to me unless I want children?'

'I don't know,' she sighed. 'I don't know why Scott married me. Some kind of status symbol, I suppose.'

'Well, let me set your mind at rest,' he said drily. 'I don't need a status symbol wife. I already have a cook and housekeeper, though I must admit I wouldn't mind your cooking for me occasionally. That was a superb meal the other night. Now what else? I certainly don't need an income-earner. Taxation is a vexing problem as it is. A resident hostess would be handy. It'd save the trouble of telephoning someone. I really can't think of any cogent reason for marriage but children. For them I do need a wife . . . and you need a husband,' he concluded with pointed emphasis.

'And what kind of relationship are we supposed to have in this marriage, apart from mothering and fathering?' she asked sceptically. 'Do you see me as constantly pregnant while you flit around the world with your mistresses?'

He grinned at her disarmingly. 'Oh, I think I've had enough footloose years to sate my appetite for variety. I'll be quite content with one woman unless you think you can't satisfy me.' His grin took on a wolfish gleam. 'Shall we go upstairs and explore the possiblity?'

She flushed, angry with herself for having been side-tracked by his talk of children. 'You're wasting your line on me, Alex. Scott decided I was frigid anyway,' she said coldly.

'There's no such thing as a frigid woman, only an inadequate lover. Men like Scott who fancy themselves as studs, rarely think of a woman's pleasure. I'd enjoy giving you pleasure, Mary Kathleen.'

Her cheeks glowed with embarrassment as his gaze roved over her speculatively. 'Will you stop that?' she demanded hotly.

'Stop what? I'm not doing a thing, except

sitting here talking to you,' he replied blandly. 'Of course if you want action, I'd be glad to oblige.'

'I don't want anything from you. Can't you get that through your head?'

'That's rather nice, you know. I really like the fact that you don't want anything from me. Money makes the world go round and usually everyone wants to hop on to the glittering carousel for a ride. It's very refreshing to meet someone who hasn't got her beady eyes glued to the main chance. Makes me want to give that person everything she wants, just for the sheer joy of giving for pleasure instead of answering greed. I think I'd like being married to you, Mary Kathleen. Why don't you marry me?'

'Because I don't want to marry anyone!' she shrilled, then held her hands to her temples to calm her agitation. 'This is a crazy conversation. I don't believe it's really happening. My husband died yesterday and you're sitting there proposing marriage. It's completely unreal and you can't mean it. It's a game, a stupid, tasteless game, and I wish you'd go away.'

He drew out some papers from the inner breast-pocket of his suit-coat and slid them down the table. 'I've signed them. Just add your signature and see how much of a game it is.'

They were marriage forms from the registry office. Kate just shook her head in disbelief. 'You're mad.'

'I doubt you'd get anyone to certify that. I'm considered very sane in business circles.'

She looked at him in helpless exasperation. 'Alex, I've just been through a rotten, degrading kind of marriage. I don't love you. I don't know you enough to even begin to trust you. Just why on earth do you think I would marry you?'

'Let's take that step by step,' he said with an air of being completely objective. 'You don't love me. Who's talking about love? I'm proposing a contract of marriage where we both agree to supply various needs, most importantly children. You had love with Scott. At least I presume you did. Something had to induce you to marry him. But you know more than I how much of a failure that was. Love's just a messy emotion which fogs up your sanity.'

'So much for love,' she commented derisively.

He pointed a finger at her and stabbed the air. 'Right! Now you did like me yesterday. Enough to trust me with your confidence. Then Scott's death muddled you up and you ran for cover.'

'I did not.'

'What would you call it?' Sharp blue eyes stripped her of any pretence. 'You've been hiding behind the institution of marriage. Rotting there actually. Suddenly you're not married any more. You've lost your protected status. I disturbed you and you ran back into a cocoon, this house. But the truth is, Mary Kathleen, you enjoyed my company yesterday and you were more honest with me than you've probably been with anyone. Why shouldn't we continue that in our marriage? No secret reserves and resentments, but good, old-fashioned plain speaking. I think that's a splendid basis for understanding. Don't you?'

She drew in a deep breath and let it out slowly, trying desperately to hang on to common sense. 'I think you have the ability to make the unreasonable sound reasonable, Alex. Even if I wanted to be your wife I'm not equipped to fit into your kind of life. I'm not a jet-set person. I'm not particularly cultured or well-educated, or even comfortable in the company of smart, sophisticated people. I'm just an ordinary typist. Why don't you pick on one of your beautiful socialites? Why me?'

'Marriage only concerns the two people in it. You and I. And I think you'll suit me better than all the socialites my mother has produced at regular intervals.'

'Your mother?'

His smile had a wry twist. 'I didn't just happen. My father is dead. My mother divorced him when I was ten and pursued her own goals in life. I ought to warn you that our marriage will be for better or worse, Mary Kathleen, till death do us part. Children don't take kindly to divorces and I shall protect my children from any threat to their sense of security.'

He was sweeping along, disregarding her negative response. 'Alex, I haven't accepted. I'm not going to accept,' she insisted. 'I don't know why I'm even discussing it with you.'

'Don't spoil it,' he demanded and sat back with a beatific smile on his face. 'I was just imagining all the little Kates and Alexs we're going to have. You'll need to stop me from spoiling them rotten. Having waited so long I'm bound to be a doting father. How many children would you like? Four? Four seems like a good number.'

It was absurd. The whole conversation was so way out that Kate began to laugh. 'Why not six, or even ten?'

'Mmmh . . . Ten plus me makes a cricket team. You can be the umpire. Do you think we can manage ten?'

She laughed until tears streamed down her face. Still with an occasional giggle emerging she sagged back in her chair and wiped her cheeks with the back of her hand.

'That's the first real laugh I've heard from you,' Alex remarked with a satisfied smile. 'You look more relaxed now.'

'So relaxed I feel like jelly,' she sighed.

'Well, I wouldn't want to spoil that pleasant feeling.' He pushed himself to his feet and strolled around the table. 'I'll go now, Kate. Telephone Peterson and Bakewell in the morning and let them work through your problems and don't worry any more. They'll give you the best advice. Just follow it.'

His voice had lost the lilt of flippancy and the teasing, probing eyes looked at her with gentle warmth. Her confusion suddenly thinned and a pure shaft of intuition burst into her mind.

'You've been distracting me, haven't you?'

He smiled. 'And been successful. You've lost that frantic, despairing look. You should sleep all right now.' His lips took on a sardonic quirk. 'After all, I've given you some nice thoughts to take to bed with you.'

'It was a game,' she concluded and was conscious of a perverse little stab of disappointment. She sighed and stood up to see him to the front door. He paused next to her as she held it open. One hand gently squeezed her shoulder and the knowing, blue eyes searched hers intently. Kate's pulse fluttered. She was suddenly

very aware of his physical impact, the huge
masculine strength of him.

'G-good night, Alex,' she stammered.

The hand on her shoulder slid up to touch her
cheek in a featherlight caress. 'I'm glad you
didn't say goodbye, Kate, because it wasn't a
game. You're going to marry me. Good night.'
His hand dropped away and he smiled. 'Dream of
our children.'

She stared after his retreating figure. He
saluted her before disappearing into his car.
Slowly, almost absently she closed the door and
walked back into the dining-room. The marriage-
forms Alex had produced were still lying on the
table. She picked them up and unfolded them.
Alex's signature leapt out at her, a sharp,
distinctive scrawl. The idea of marrying Alex
Dalton wormed around in her mind for several
minutes before she abruptly banished it, telling
herself it was crazy.

She switched off the light and headed upstairs,
exhaustion dragging her steps. It was a relief to
climb into bed but her mind was too active to
allow a soothing drift into sleep. It seemed a
bitter reflection on her married life that of all the
people who had visited her today, so-called
friends and relatives, it had been Alex Dalton, a
complete outsider, who had supplied her with the
direction she needed, the names of a good
accountant and solicitor. Tomorrow she would be
able to make an effective start on clearing up
Scott's estate. She would get rid of all his
personal possessions, too. Today she had felt
emotionally battered but tomorrow she would act
with more purpose.

Despite her resolution to put Alex's proposal
out of her mind it niggled around the edges of her
thoughts until she gave it entry. Her marriage to
Scott had become a prison and Kate had no
intention of walking out of one cage into another,
however gilded it looked. She wanted to be
herself, not someone else's possession. And yet
... if she was ever to be a mother ... hold her
own baby in her arms ... A whole tribe of
children at progressive ages marched through her
mind, and behind them came Alex Dalton with a
cricket bat and a proudly paternal look on his
face.

Kate's mouth curved into a faint smile. It was
pure fantasy and unfortunately reality never
matched fantasy. Her dreams had never blos-
somed. Scott had cut them down with callous
disregard until her soul had filled with grey
nothingness. Alex had stirred those dreams to life
again but Kate was too sceptical to believe they
could come true.

The next two days were extremely busy ones
but Kate had the satisfaction of knowing they
were productive. She was surprised and grateful
to obtain immediate appointments with Carl
Peterson and Steven Bakewell. The accountant
skimmed through Scott's papers, arranged a
meeting with Terry Jessell and promised to work
out a list of financial options for her by the end of
the week. The solicitor was equally impressive,
assuring her that he would arrange the transfer of
Scott's legal documents from Bob Chardway and
that she would be informed of the situation as
soon as he had the facts in hand.

She gave Scott's clothes to a charitable

organisation for the needy. There were some personal mementos which she put aside to give to his parents but everything else was ruthlessly disposed of. A second-hand dealer bought the sporting equipment and the few knick-knacks left were consigned to the rubbish bin.

On Wednesday night she sat through a duty dinner with Scott's parents. The funeral arrangements were hashed over again. Sheila Andrews wept copious tears over the photograph albums and sporting trophies Kate had given her. Harry Andrews mouthed concern about Kate's future without coming to grips with anything constructive. Kate did not care. She wanted to sever all contact with the Andrews family. Scott had been their blue-eyed boy and she had long ago lost any empathy with them.

The funeral itself was an ordeal. The service was mercifully brief but the trip to the crematorium and the sympathetic gushing from Scott's friends and relatives tested her composure. Their words were completely empty. Harry Andrews called her a brave little woman but her dry eyes had nothing to do with bravery. In fact her calm façade hid a seething impatience for it all to be over.

When at last she was alone in the house she felt a vast relief. In a sudden spurt of rebellion she threw off her widow's garb and dressed in jeans and T-shirt. The smooth conservative French pleat was unpinned and her hair raked free of confinement. Kate was finished with confinement of any kind. From now on her life was her own.

It was only after she had defiantly downed a large sherry that she really sat down and considered her future. She was not a career-person. All she had ever wanted to do was get married and raise a family. The idea of spending the rest of her life typing was not very attractive. Her gaze travelled around the lounge, recognising that this comfort would be very short-lived. The house had to be sold to cover outstanding debts and much of the furniture would be repossessed. There was no way she could keep up the hire-purchase payments.

She was about to pour herself another sherry when the doorbell rang. The bottle almost slipped from her hand. She did not want another visitor. The mourning charade was over as far as she was concerned. The doorbell kept ringing. Annoyed by the intrusion Kate tweeked the curtains enough to peer outside. Alex Dalton's Lamborghini stood at the kerb. Relief poured through her. No pretence was necessary with Alex. Resigned to the certainty that he would not go away, Kate answered the door.

He surveyed her with open amusement. 'The funeral is obviously over.'

'You missed it,' she said wryly.

'You could call me many things, Mary Kathleen, but not a hypocrite.'

He stepped past her, not waiting for an invitation to enter. She shut the door and waved him into the lounge.

'I'm having a drink. At least I was when you interrupted me.'

'I'll join you.'

He dropped into an armchair and watched her pour the drinks. 'You know, you have the perfect figure for wearing T-shirts,' he observed appreciatively.

Kate flushed, belatedly remembering that she had removed her bra along with her other black clothes. 'I wasn't expecting any more visitors. Why did you come, Alex?'

'To take you out to dinner.'

His conservative business-suit added to his characteristic air of confident maturity. Kate looked at him and saw solidity and security. It was a powerful combination, more so because they were the qualities which Scott had lacked. With sudden insight Kate realised that if she ever married again, these were the very qualities she would instinctively look for in a husband.

'Do you still want to marry me?' she asked bluntly.

A sharp alertness snapped into his eyes. 'That was behind the dinner invitation.'

'We enter a contract. Is that right? We make agreements which we're both prepared to keep?' she said with slow deliberation, feeling out the words as she spoke.

'Correct,' he nodded.

'All right then. We'll go out to dinner and work out our agreements, but I'll have one point straight right now. I won't tolerate your making any sexual advances to me before we're married. It's marriage or nothing. Do you understand me, Alex?'

'Implicitly,' he said with a sardonic smile. 'You don't trust my word.'

She sighed. 'I've been through a hard school and there's very little I'll take on faith any more. I won't be tricked into becoming your mistress.'

A weary mockery carved itself into his expression. 'I'm quite prepared to wait until you'll be sharing my bed legally, but share it then you will, Kate, every night of our married lives. Let that be clear between us too.'

'Since having a family is our mutual goal I can hardly argue against that,' she said levelly, but she was a little shaken by the ruthless tone in his voice.

She had not given any thought to the intimacy of marriage when she had made her spur-of-the-moment decision. She had merely looked ahead and made a pragmatic choice. At almost twenty-eight years of age Kate knew that time was running out if she wanted a family and she did not expect to fall in love again. Alex not only wanted children, he could provide them with every advantage. She bolstered her resolve with the thought that going to bed with him could not be any worse than sleeping with Scott after she had learnt of his infidelities.

At least there would be purpose in this marriage. She did not love Alex but his children would also be hers and she could give them all the stifled love in her heart. She would make a good future within this marriage and she would not repeat the mistake of depending on her husband for happiness. Since her emotions were not involved with Alex, he could not hurt her as Scott had. Maybe that was an advantage. In any case she had made her decision and she would stick to it. It was a positive step.

CHAPTER SEVEN

'I NOW pronounce you man and wife.'

Kate swallowed and lifted her chin a little higher. It was done. They were married.

'Just sign here, Mrs Dalton.'

A clerk held a pen out to her. She took it and concentrated on performing the last requirement for their contract to become legal.

'Mr Dalton?'

Alex dashed off his signature. The clerks who had acted as witnesses added theirs. The marriage certificate was folded up and handed to Kate. She put it in her handbag and looked up at her new husband, determined to quell the nervous flutter in her stomach.

'Do we shake hands when a contract is signed, sealed and delivered?'

He smiled. 'I think you've done enough shaking this morning.' He tucked her arm into his and began walking her out to the warming sunshine. 'Feeling better?'

'Was it so obvious?'

'That you were screwing your courage to the sticking point?'

She gave a shaky little laugh. 'Well, it was quite a step.'

'And I'm glad your courage didn't slip.'

She glanced up at him defensively. 'I wouldn't have backed out. I keep my promises, Alex.'

His eyes held hers. 'So do I, Mary Kathleen. So do I.'

He had kept them so far. Kate could not quibble about that. The sexual ban she had insisted upon had been strictly adhered to. Alex had not even attempted the slightest infringement. Perversely enough it had been this total lack of sexual communication which had put her into a flat panic this morning. All the calculated advantages in their marriage had suddenly faded into insignificance beside the one looming certainty that tonight she had to sleep with him.

The binding, lifelong contract had now been signed. Alex's relaxed manner had a calming effect but still her thoughts kept zeroing in on one image. Bed. It stifled her appetite at the celebratory lunch Alex insisted upon. It flew with her on the flight to Tasmania. It invaded the taxi on their way to the hotel-casino in Hobart. It stared her in the face when they were shown into their hotel-suite. Late that night it filled the mirror as she sat at the dressing-table brushing her hair.

One hundred, two, three ... not even a thousand strokes would take away the inevitability of what had to follow. She knew Alex was watching her but she could not meet his gaze in the mirror. Her eyes had skittered away from his reflected image ever since he had discarded his bathrobe. She had not anticipated his climbing into bed stark naked. She had kept brushing her hair in a vain attempt to soothe the panic which had swept through her veins. With firm resolve she put the hairbrush down.

They were married. She had made promises

which had to be fulfilled. There was no point in postponing the consummation of a marriage she had walked into of her own free will. Her skin felt clammy with apprehension but she forced herself to stand up and take off the silk and lace négligée. The nightie she had chosen clung seductively to her curves but it was not transparent. Holding tightly to a façade of calm unconcern she walked over to the vacant side of the bed and lifted back the bedclothes.

'That's a very pretty nightie, Kate, but I won't appreciate it in bed. Scott might have preferred silk to skin but I don't,' he stated casually.

She looked at him then. He lay there completely relaxed, his hands behind his head, eyes observing her with cynical amusement.

'Then you can take it off, can't you?' she retorted, pride insisting that she hide the nervous fear which was knotting her stomach.

'Much easier for you to do it now.'

'I don't want to. You might like to go to bed with nothing on but I don't.'

She switched off her bedside light and slid between the sheets. Alex made no move to turn his light off. He rolled on to his side, casually propping his head up on one hand and looking down at her with mocking eyes.

'How extraordinary! Do you mean to tell me you've worn a nightie to bed every night of your life?'

'Not every night,' she replied silkily. 'Sometimes I wore pyjamas.'

He grinned, clearly enjoying himself. 'And did you always make love in the dark?'

Her throat dried up as she realised he had no

intention of turning out his light. 'No,' she forced out, determined to pretend she did not care.

'I'm glad you have no objection to light. I like to indulge all my senses. It's so much more satisfying. Touch, for instance. You have such fine, delicate skin.' His fingers caressed the line of her throat and shoulders, trailed down the V-neckline of her nightie, then probed under the silk to gently circle her breasts. 'Exquisite! I've wanted to feel its texture since the first night we met.'

Kate could not repress a little shiver.

He smiled. 'Then there's taste. Despite all the bitterness which has dripped from your tongue there is something extremely sweet about forbidden fruit. It was unwise of you to forbid me your body, Kate. When a man is frustrated he builds up a greed and I'm greedy for the softness of your mouth.'

She froze as his lips brushed teasingly against hers, nibbling at their stiffness with gentle persistence until curiosity prompted her to fully experience his kiss. He took full advantage of her pliancy, exploring her mouth with extraordinary sensuality. Kate had never been kissed with such thorough expertise and she was surprised to find how pleasant it was. She would have liked it to go on, tempted to examine the sensations he was arousing but he withdrew to graze his lips over her face, moving slowly upwards to her temples.

'Mmmmh. Your hair smells faintly of lemons. Smell is the most subtle sense of all, endlessly teasing with its complexities.'

His breath wavered through her hair and for a moment Kate was entranced with his gentleness.

Then abruptly he drew back and looked down at her, a wicked gleam of satisfaction in his eyes.

'But tonight, my sweet Kate, I especially want to indulge the sense of sight, and your nightie is decidedly superfluous.'

She struggled, instinctively resisting the vulnerability of nakedness. He laughed and she stopped, forcing herself into passivity. He lifted the flimsy garment over her head and tossed it on the floor. With one sweep of the hand he dispensed with the bedclothes. Kate gritted her teeth, willing herself not to flinch under his gaze. Goose-bumps prickled over her skin and her heart wildly protested his visual assault on her body.

'Why do you need to hide such loveliness?' he demanded huskily. There was an avid possessiveness in his touch as his hand followed the path of his gaze. 'A truly feminine body, soft thighs, hips beautifully rounded and your breasts . . . I envy our children the pleasure they'll have.'

He leaned over and rolled his tongue around each nipple. Kate tensed, electrified by the sweet wave of pleasure which rippled through her. His hand caressed her inner thighs, gently prising them apart. She gasped and jerked away as he touched her intimately. He instantly shifted his position, his mouth claiming hers with more passionate demand while one strongly muscled leg moved to prevent any resistance to his erotic play.

Kate was helplessly pinned under his weight and the skilled assault on her senses continued relentlessly. A melting weakness invaded her body. Nerve-ends quivered and jumped erratically until Kate felt she would explode with the mounting tension. Her body seemed to be at war with itself, demanding a release she could not supply.

'You have to want me, Kate,' Alex murmured against her lips. Then his mouth roamed downwards, leaving a chaos of sensitivity in its wake.

She clutched at his shoulders, her fingers kneading the strong muscles in agonised protest. 'Please . . . I . . .' The words tore from her throat, driven out by a primitive compulsion which could not be denied.

'Now?'

'Yes . . . yes . . .' she moaned.

'Then make me feel wanted. Kiss me back. Touch me. Need me with your body.'

Almost mindless with the urgency of her desire she responded with feverish eagerness, giving him whatever he demanded until their need for mutual possession could no longer be contained. She sighed with ecstatic pleasure as they joined and the pleasure bloomed, spreading its warm, triumphant glow through her whole body. It magnified, new ripples of sensation bursting over those ebbing until Kate was swamped with such a flood of feeling that nothing else existed.

At last came the shuddering appeasement of every need and even when satisfaction was gloriously complete, they clung on to intimacy, unwilling to let go that incredible togetherness. It was a long time before Kate stirred and then it was only to touch Alex's body in tentative wonder, amazed that it could have given her such pleasure.

His hand moved in a slow caress up her spine. Fingers threaded through her hair, took a grip on the long tresses and gently pulled her head back. His lips brushed lazily against hers, provoking a tingling buzz of feeling until her mouth opened willingly under his. It was a beautiful kiss, harmonising with the satisfied hum of their languid bodies. She nestled her head back under his chin, knowing a sexual contentment she had never known before.

A soft chuckle rumbled up from his chest, amusement, pleasure and satisfaction in the sound. 'Yes, I think we'll serve each other very well,' he murmured against her hair.

His hand slid back down the curve of her back, reinforcing the possession in his voice. Kate made no reply. The marriage was consummated, the commitment made final, and she was happily relieved to find no regrets in her heart. Added to all his other attractive qualities was the undeniable fact that Alex was a generous lover. She counted herself very lucky indeed to have such a husband as father for her future children.

Why Alex had chosen her for his wife was a question which still niggled at her mind. It rose again now but she did not voice it. Alex had never satisfactorily answered it and she guessed he would only turn it aside with some flippant remark as he had done on other occasions. Provided he kept to the terms of their contract she did not need to know his motives.

In fact, Kate had questioned very little. Once she had given her consent Alex had swept her into marriage without any regard for social conventions. It was only five weeks since Scott's death. There had been no family meetings, no introduction to friends, no publicity of any kind. The month prior to their wedding had been spent exclusively in each other's company. Alex had coolly stated that he preferred to present a fait accompli to family and friends and their marriage was nobody's business but their own.

Kate had clung single-mindedly to the course she had chosen, refusing to let any doubts worry her. She argued to herself that as Alex's wife she would be automatically accepted by the society in which he moved. Alex had the strength of personality to ensure that. In any case it was not important to her. She would have her children.

She had told no one in Sydney of her marriage plans. Her employer had accepted her resignation with tactful regret and Scott's friends had quickly dropped all contact with her. Only her father had been informed. Alex had announced they would have a week to themselves at the luxurious hotel-casino in Hobart, after which she could introduce him to her family. The yacht was to be sailed down by the crew and they would proceed to a two-week cruise around New Zealand.

Kate had accepted his plans without demur. It would be good to see her own family again after five years of separation. Apart from that Kate only had one wish, to become pregnant. Maybe tonight she had already conceived she thought hopefully, and drifted into sleep with a smile on her lips.

A physical sense of cold unfamiliarity jarred her awake. It was morning. She was naked. The memory of last night whipped through her mind and she quickly turned her head. Alex was not beside her. She wondered how late it was and quickly scrambled out of bed, her feet landing on the discarded nightie. She snatched it up and pulled it over her head, feeling more comfortable with clothing on.

Alex was in the sitting-room of their suite. He was clean-shaven and fully dressed in light blue linen slacks and a casual knit-shirt. A newspaper was absorbing his attention. A half-full glass of tomato juice sat on a table near his elbow. Obviously he had been up for some time and Kate felt awkward about having overslept. She vacillated over whether to greet him, finally deciding to wash and dress first. She was soaping herself under the shower when the glass door slid open.

'Hi!'

She gaped at Alex, the friendly grin on his face doing nothing to lessen the embarrassment which flooded heat over her skin.

'You slept well. Shall I order breakfast?'

'Yes . . . please,' she added quickly, wishing he would go away. The gleam in his eyes vividly recalled last night's intimacy.

'Bacon and eggs?'

'Yes, yes, anything.'

His grin widened. 'Might as well get used to it, Kate. We're going to be married for a long time.'

'I . . . I was just about to get out,' she said, hurriedly fumbling with the taps. 'Would you pass me a towel, please?'

He held it for her so that she had to step out of the shower cabinet with nothing to hide her nakedness. She felt hopelessly vulnerable. The lack of clothes stripped her of any protection, physically and mentally.

'Why are you so inhibited?' he asked as he wrapped the towel around her. 'You should be proud of your lovely body.'

Her lashes flickered up and a mute plea shone out of her eyes. His hand touched her cheek in a gentle caress and his expression softened.

'You have nothing to fear from me, Kate. Don't hide.'

'Am I to have no privacy, Alex?' she asked defensively, her cheeks burning with the effort to mentally fend him off. She did not want him jabbing at sensitive areas which held the memory of too much hurt.

His hand slid down to her chin, lifting it for his eyes to probe hers. 'Some wounds need fresh air to heal. I don't want anything from your previous marriage festering between us, Kate. Forget Scott. This is you and me and I like your body. I like seeing you naked, the delicate tones of your skin and the soft, feminine contours. It gives me pleasure. Doesn't it please you to be admired?'

'Alex . . .'

His other hand freed the towel and it dropped to the floor. Panic jabbed at her nerves but she resisted the impulse to snatch it back up.

'That's not fair,' she declared tightly. 'You're dressed.'

'I'm just as comfortable in my skin. Why aren't you? Do you equate nakedness with sex? Is sex still a dirty word to you?'

'I never said it was a dirty word.'

'No, but you didn't expect to enjoy yourself last night. Do you find it shameful that you did?'

His finger ran slowly down to the valley between her breasts and paused there. Her breath caught in her throat. Her heart thumped a wild tattoo against her chest.

'No. Why should I?' she croaked out in a defiant rush. 'I'm just as entitled to enjoy myself as you are.'

It was a slow grin, gathering satisfaction as it widened. 'So you are, my fiery Kate, so you are. Hold on to that thought. I'll order breakfast while you dress.' His finger trailed down to her navel before dropping away as he turned.

Kate released her breath in a shuddering sigh then reached for the towel. There was no need for it. Her skin was dry. She examined her reflection in the mirror, considering her body anew in the light of Alex's remarks. Scott had viewed it with contempt. His sneering comments writhed through her memory like poisonous snakes: 'the frigid corpse; virgin mentality wrapped in snow-white skin; veined like marble and just as lifeless.' Clothes had been a defensive shield against his cruel jibes.

But she was not frigid and Alex liked her body. Looked at objectively it really was a nice body, well-proportioned, not voluptuous but pleasantly rounded. She had sometimes wished for larger breasts but hers were firm and ... perfect for wearing T-shirts. She smiled as she recalled Alex's words. She believed he had meant what he said. The confidence Scott had crushed began creeping back. It was pleasant to be married to a man who really liked you. She had thought Alex callous, but he had shown he cared about her feelings. A warm glow lightened her heart.

And last night ... no, she wasn't at all ashamed of anything that happened last night. Alex's lovemaking had been a sexual revelation to her, a little frightening at first but then . . . such an incredible feeling. She ran a hand over her stomach trying to recall the delicious nuances of that feeling. It was impossible. Maybe tonight . . . she flushed at the wanton thought and hurried into the bedroom to dress.

'Oh, by the way,' Alex called out from the sitting-room, 'I'm taking you shopping for clothes. Please yourself how you dress. I just thought I'd warn you.'

Kate paused, a pair of slacks in her hands. 'What kind of clothes?' she asked with a frown. 'I don't think I need anything.'

Alex strolled in and lazily stretched his length on the bed, hands behind his head, eyes surveying her with a teasing gleam. 'Not underclothes. Those are very fetching. Actually clothes don't interest me much but I know what women are like, very competitive when it comes to the fashion scene. I don't want my mother or her society friends making you feel inferior. Unlike your astute husband they'll only see what's on the surface and so, my dear wife, we'll armour you against their bitchiness.'

'Wife' was the operative word. Kate suddenly realised that she was bound to be looked at critically. Alex had married her and everyone would speculate on why. 'Is that why you didn't introduce me to anyone? Because of my clothes?' she asked sharply.

'No. I didn't want you scared off our marriage,' he answered with off-hand directness. 'However, I have no delusions about my mother. She can be a formidable adversary. She won't approve of you, Kate, not as my wife. I don't give a damn what she thinks and I hope you're of like mind. Still, it might be easier for you fitted out in the finest feathers.'

'I see,' she said stiffly, looking at her clothes with newly critical eyes. They were not haute couture by any stretch of imagination. She sighed and murmured, 'That's very considerate of you, Alex.'

'Just practical. You don't mind shopping, do you? I thought all women loved clothes,' he remarked dryly.

Kate zipped on her best day-dress and smoothed it over her hips, wishing it was better cut. 'No, I don't mind. It's your idea and you're paying for them. I dare say Alex Dalton's wife should look the part, but I'm not going to let your mother or anyone else bother me.' Her chin came up in proud defiance. 'I married you to have a family and that's what I'll have, no matter what clothes I wear.'

He grinned. 'That's what I like. Strength of character. Maybe we should forgo breakfast and work on starting a family.'

'I'm hungry,' she declared and turned to the drawer which contained her tights as a betraying blush stained her cheeks.

'Then we won't forgo breakfast. A rumbling stomach is not conducive to good sex,' he said equably.

'You ought to know,' she breathed.

'Pardon?'

She darted him a shy glance as she bent down to roll on her tights. 'I just meant you're a very good lover.'

'What every bridegroom likes to hear,' he said with a sardonic lilt. Then in a softer voice, 'You're quite something yourself once you let go, Mary Kathleen.'

Her skin prickled with the memory of her abandoned response. She found the right shoes and slipped them on before turning around. His gaze was oddly calculating and she shrugged away the unspoken question with a rueful smile. 'I didn't know it could be like that.'

He nodded. 'Those five years with Scott must have been five years of backward steps, a lot of damage to be undone. Come here.' He took a hand from behind his head and held it out in a beckoning gesture.

'What . . . what do you want?'

'You.'

'I'm dressed. Breakfast . . . you don't like rumbling stomachs,' she said jerkily, instinctively denying her own desire, not willing to become a slave to him, not for any reason.

'I'm not going to kiss your stomach.' His legs swung down and he stood up. 'Don't expect me always to take the initiative, Kate. I'll lose interest in a sexually passive partner. Meet me halfway. That's the bargain we made.'

His demanding stance was a deliberate challenge.

'What's the point in kissing?' she protested.

'Is a kiss so difficult to give?'

She shook her head, feeling a little foolish for being so awkward about it.

'Well?'

Kate forced herself to walk over and slide her arms around his neck. Stronger arms swept her hard against him and before she had time to question, his mouth claimed hers with masterly persuasion. Her first tentative response quickly gave way to wholehearted fervour as hands sensually moulded her to his hard masculinity. Passion stirred and only when the doorbell echoed jarringly in her ears did Kate realise that her fingers were thrust into the short thickness of Alex's hair, blindly urging more intimacy. She abruptly pulled away, confused by the strength of her reaction.

'The ... the waiter ... breakfast,' she stammered.

'I could easily get addicted to "good morning" kisses from my wife,' Alex murmured, one finger lightly brushing her throbbing lips. Then with a whimsical little smile curving his mouth he slid an arm around her shoulders and drew her with him into the sitting-room.

He saw her seated at the table before answering the door. Breakfast was wheeled in and served by a cheerful waiter. Kate barely heard his lively patter. All the lessons she had learnt from the past were cramming into one warning message: don't become emotionally dependent on Alex Dalton. So he was a good lover. Accept and enjoy the physical pleasure for what it was—a response to expert stimulation. Don't let it mean any more than that.

'You're very pensive. What are you thinking?'

Kate glanced up warily. The waiter had gone and Alex was seating himself opposite her. She realised he was still a stranger to her in many ways, despite the fact he was her husband. In keeping her own tight reserve she had not even attempted to probe his. What lay beneath the civilised veneer was as much a mystery to her now as it was the night they met.

'I don't really know much about you, do I, Alex?'

'You haven't been inclined to question. What do you want to know?'

'I'm not sure I want to know anything in particular.' She shrugged. 'It was just a thought.'

'Is ignorance bliss?' he mocked.

'It's better than bad news.'

She began eating her breakfast but looked up in surprise when he chuckled. She raised her eyebrows, questioning his amusement.

'You make an admirable wife, Mary Kathleen. Very Victorian.'

She swallowed her food and remarked, 'Well, it is a marriage of convenience.'

'And very convenient it is. I'm liking it better all the time.' After which statement he gave his full attention to breakfast.

Kate was content to let the conversation drop. Alex's good humour was tainted with cynicism but at least he had never shown a streak of meanness. What she knew of him she liked and that was enough to know. Too much knowledge might be unsettling.

CHAPTER EIGHT

'ALEX! What are you doing here?' Surprise and pleasure trilled in a warm purr as a very svelte blonde clutched Alex's shoulder.

'Dining out,' he answered matter-of-factly. 'How are you, Sonia?'

'Exhausted, darling . . .'

Kate watched curiously as the woman started detailing the modelling assignment which was keeping her busy. This woman obviously shared the same social circle as Alex. She was polished with a sophisticated elegance which made Kate appreciate Alex's point about clothes. She was suddenly glad that the dress she was wearing tonight was a designer-model. And yet Alex was still not introducing her. He sat with a half-smile on his face, ignoring the pointed glances which Sonia darted towards Kate.

'. . . Nicole told me you'd gone away but I assumed you'd tripped off overseas. What brought you to New Zealand? Business?' A more pointed glance was directed at Kate this time.

'No. Strictly pleasure.'

'Oh?' One finely arched eyebrow rose higher and she stared directly at Kate, determined on an introduction.

Alex sighed and tapped his fingers on the table in an irritable manner. 'It is, of course, always a pleasure to see you, Sonia, but at the moment you are intruding. My wife and I are still on our honeymoon.'

'Your . . . wife?' The incredulity in her voice was reflected in her eyes as she looked from Kate to Alex and back again.

'Kate, may I introduce Sonia Benelle. Sonia, my wife, Kate.'

'How do you do?' Kate murmured politely.

Sonia was having difficulty articulating a word. She swallowed and licked her lips as she stared at Kate. Then abruptly she turned back to Alex. 'Your wife?' she repeated in a hollow voice.

'Correct . . . for the second time,' he added dryly.

'My God! Does Nicole know?' Sonia demanded, almost gasping for breath.

'I'm sure you'll tell her, Sonia. Now, if you don't mind . . .'

'But . . .'

'Kate and I would prefer to be alone,' Alex finished coldly.

Sonia stared at Kate again, this time with the keen appraisal of a competitor. 'Congratulations,' she said on a sour note. 'To you both,' she added belatedly, a brittle smile pasted on her face. She backed away then spun on her heel and hurried out of the dining-room.

Alex twirled the claret around in his glass, examined the colour with a critical eye, then tasted it slowly, giving the process all the ceremony of a wine connoisseur making a judgment. 'Not a bad year. Should improve with age,' he declared sardonically.

'If there's not too much turbulance ahead. Apparently that was quite a bombshell you just dropped. Who is Nicole?' she asked bluntly, fighting to dismiss the fear which had begun crawling around her heart.

Alex's face showed nothing. It was as if shutters had been pulled down and clicked into place. They were labelled Private—No Admittance. His gaze remained fixed on the claret as he tipped his glass backwards and forwards. 'Nicole Fouvet is the woman I was expected to marry.'

He said it so casually, like a throw-away line, but Kate was not deceived. Her intuition was prickling alarmingly. The question which had teased her mind suddenly took on an added dimension. Why had he married her instead of Nicole Fouvet? The woman meant something to him and the relationship had to have been serious to account for Sonia's reaction.

'Will she be as surprised about our marriage as your friend, Sonia?' Kate probed cautiously.

'Maybe,' he shrugged, then flicked her a derisive look. 'I anticipate that a lot of people will be surprised. Now that the news is out, the reaction at home should be quite interesting. My mother will undoubtedly arrange one of her Evenings for us and you, my dear Kate, will be given star billing. Are you ready to cope with the curiosity?'

'With your support.'

A touch of grimness settled around his mouth. 'You'll always have that, Kate. I keep my promises.'

She nodded. Alex had given her no reason to doubt that. However, she wondered how their relationship would stand up in the day-to-day reality of married life.

Their honeymoon was at an end. This was their last night in New Zealand waters. Tomorrow they were sailing for home. Kate worried over the name, Nicole Fouvet, as she sliced off a piece of French walnut cheese. In a way she wished Alex had not brought her to this restaurant, reputedly the best in Auckland. She had been happy until Sonia Benelle had dropped that name.

'Why didn't you marry her?'

Alex did not answer. He leaned back in his chair, his heavy-lidded gaze denying her access to his thoughts. 'It's been a good three weeks. I've enjoyed your company, Mary Kathleen.'

Kate frowned. His use of her full name always irritated her. It came at oddly chosen moments and she was never sure what prompted its use.

'I enjoyed meeting your family,' Alex continued. 'I liked your father . . . a strong, straight kind of man. Your stepmother seems a nice woman too and your half-brothers and sisters are delightful kids. I regret that my own mother will not welcome you as warmly as I was welcomed by your family.'

Kate gave him a wry smile. 'I don't have as much to give.'

Alex had entertained her family in an extravagant fashion, a day-trip on the yacht, gifts, dinner at the casino. They had been more than a little dazzled by his wealth.

'I consider our marriage the best contract I ever signed. I hope you have no regrets,' he said with a touch of concern.

She shook her head. Alex had given her no reason to regret their marriage. It had taken her several days to relax in his constant company.

Her initial awkwardness had dissolved as she had come to accept that Alex meant exactly what he said. He was considerate, generous, good company, in bed and out of it. She could not complain about anything.

'You're happy with me?' The blue eyes probed hers, intent on piercing her defensive shell.

Yes, she had been happy, happier than she had any right to expect considering the terms of their contract. There had been times when she felt very much in danger of falling in love with him. Her caution about becoming emotionally involved was now vindicated by his evasive silence on the subject of Nicole Fouvet.

'Is that so difficult to answer?' he asked dryly.

She glanced up, a self-conscious flush on her cheeks. 'I appreciate, very much, how good you've been to me.'

'Kate . . .' He stopped and the sudden flare in his eyes died as he let out a long sigh. He leaned forward, reached across the table and took her left hand in his, fingering the rings he had placed there. 'You won't give in, will you?' he said broodingly. 'Scott did too good a job on you, the bastard. I'm going to wear all those barriers down if it's the last Goddamned thing I do.'

The quiet ferocity in his voice made her shiver. She tried to extract her hand but he held it fast. His eyes held hers even more determinedly.

'I want all of you, Kate, and I won't be satisfied with less.'

'No,' she whispered, shaking her head in mute protest. 'Don't, Alex. Don't spoil it.'

'What am I spoiling?'

A tumult of feeling had broken out of a tightly

locked compartment in her heart. It confused and frightened her. She was too vulnerable to the power he was exerting. 'I'm happy with you,' she said in a frantic rush, saying the words which she thought might satisfy his demand.

'But you don't expect it to last. You stand back, encircling yourself with the protection of independence. What do you think I'll do? I'm not a Jekyll and Hyde character. You can trust me, Mary Kathleen,' he added with soft persuasion.

She closed her eyes against the steady onslaught of his gaze. Maybe he could be trusted but only time would prove that to her. Their honeymoon had been no real test of trustworthiness. Betrayal only came with temptation. Maybe with Nicole Fouvet. And yet Alex seemed a man of his word. She gritted her teeth against weakening and looked at him guardedly. 'I trust you to keep to the terms of our contract, Alex.'

'There was no limiting clause in our contract. It held the minimum terms for our marriage to become fact. We could improve on them.'

'I'm satisfied with what we have.'

'Completely?'

'It's enough.'

'And more would be dangerous.'

She flinched from his accurate perception. 'What are you fishing for, Alex? You claimed that you wanted no messy emotions in our marriage.'

He retreated, letting her hand slip away as he relaxed back in his chair. 'So I did,' he murmured with dry self-mockery. 'Unfortunately I have a weakness for challenges and a compulsion to win. Forgive me, Kate. I understand your lack of trust but I find it oddly offensive applied to me.'

'I'm sorry. I . . .'

'No, don't apologise. There's no obligation to give me any more than we agreed upon.'

A blush of shame scorched across her cheeks. Alex had given her far more than they had agreed upon. 'I have to survive in my own way, Alex,' she muttered in self-conscious explanation.

'Yes, it's a hard game, survival. Makes one ruthless.' He suddenly smiled at her, relaxing the tension. 'Would you like to order dessert now?'

'I've had enough, thank you.'

She was relieved that he was not pursuing this argument. Since their marriage he had probed and pushed, sometimes gently, sometimes with relentless purpose, always intent on winning his way. Kate could not deny that their relationship was the better for his manipulation. He had freed her from many little fears, boosted her confidence, shown her a respect which raised her self-esteem. She was grateful to him and gladly gave him her body, but her soul she held grimly to her own safe-keeping. Alex did not love her. He did not seem to need love. His ego was a little piqued that she would not totally surrender to him but he had the self-honesty to concede that.

'Have I been too ruthless with you, Kate?' he asked softly and she glanced up into eyes which held a wry tenderness.

'No, I was just thinking that you've administered a lot of effective medicine. I was a mass of nerves when you married me.'

'But now you're ready to spit the world in its eye.'

She smiled. 'Not quite, but I won't suffer from

dry throat. Thank you for the rescue operation, Alex,' she said sincerely.

'My pleasure. I like what we now have together. It's good, Kate. Better than I thought possible.'

'I feel the same way.'

'Strange how things work out,' he mused. 'I coldly calculated this marriage.'

'So did I.'

The band tuned up to play another bracket of songs and the main vocalist took the microphone. He had a husky, crooning voice which was pleasant without demanding rapt attention.

'Let's dance,' Alex suggested, and in his very male, arrogant way, did not wait for a reply.

The small dance-floor was already crowded. The tempo of the song was slow and most of the couples were barely swaying. Alex's arms gathered her in and Kate readily succumbed to the pleasure of feeling the strongly muscled thighs brush against hers. She slid her hands around his neck and he smiled down at her, desire kindling in his eyes. She smiled back, acknowledging the answering flare in her own veins. His hands pressed lower.

'Why don't we skip coffee and go back to the yacht?' he murmured wickedly.

'Why don't we?'

She no longer tried to deny the sensual hunger he had awakened in her. She savoured every minute of their lovemaking. It was everything she had ever imagined it could be and more. Much, much later, in the afterglow of a complete sexual satisfaction and with Alex's arms still cradling her against him, Kate marvelled over the physical harmony she shared with this man, her husband.

Alex delighted in the sense of touch and only in sleep did he ever turn away from her. She remembered how Scott had always disengaged himself once his sexual need had been satisfied. Kate's needs had never counted with him. Alex, on the other hand, was not content unless both of them shared the same peak of excitement and he savoured their intimacy long after satisfaction had been given and taken. For this experience alone she was glad she had married him, but another secret happiness bubbled in her heart. Her monthly cycle had been broken. She was seven days overdue and she felt sure a baby had been conceived.

'Alex,' she whispered.

'Mmmmh?' he murmured sleepily.

No, not now, she decided quickly. It was better to wait until she was absolutely certain. 'Oh, nothing,' she sighed and snuggled closer. 'Just happy.'

'Mmmh . . . nice,' he breathed against her hair and his hand languorously stroked her body in soft emphasis.

A wonderful sense of well-being spread through Kate. Maybe it was foolish to hold back her feelings for Alex. Maybe . . . no. She had to learn about Nicole Fouvet. Until Kate understood Alex's motives for marrying her it would be foolishly premature to surrender to him. There was too much she did not know and now she wanted to know, needed to know.

Three days later they sailed through the Heads of Sydney Harbour. Within hours Kate found their honeymoon was over with a vengeance. Her introduction to Alex's housekeeper brought the first glimmering of what was to come.

The woman was fiftyish with iron-grey hair netted in a tight bun, a lined, weather-beaten face and a stoutish figure carried by a very straight back. Her shrewd hazel eyes appraised Kate warily as Alex gave instructions in his usual authoritative manner.

'I'll show my wife over the house first. We'll have coffee in the garden room in half an hour, Mrs Beatty, and dinner at seven.'

'I hope you'll find everything to your satisfaction, Mrs Dalton,' the housekeeper said stiffly. 'Please let me know if there's anything you want done.'

'Thank you, Mrs Beatty,' Kate smiled, hoping that she would be able to make friends with the woman who had served Alex for five years.

'And, Mr Dalton, Mrs Pallister has left many messages for you to telephone her as soon as you come home.'

'I'm sure she has,' Alex commented dryly. 'I'll get around to it, Mrs Beatty.'

'What should I say if she rings again?'

'I'll take the call.'

'Very well, Mr Dalton,' she nodded and marched away.

Kate sighed and gave Alex a tentative smile. 'I guess she'll get used to me.'

'Don't worry. I've no doubt Mrs Beatty will clasp you to her ample bosom once she gets to know you. Upstairs first?'

They were still standing in the foyer where the housekeeper had welcomed them. The floor was Italian marble and an elaborate chandelier hung from the high ceiling. Kate took a deep breath and headed for the impressive staircase which rose in a sweeping curve to the upper floor. The balustrade was of white aluminium lace, very ornate. The steps were covered in thick, dove-grey carpet. Kate was very aware of entering a world of luxury and wealth.

'Who's Mrs Pallister?' she asked.

'My mother. After she divorced my father she married again. Pallister died of a heart attack some years ago.'

'You've hardly spoken of your father, Alex.'

He gave a heavy sigh and Kate glanced at him curiously. A sad weariness dragged at the lines of his face.

'Dad killed himself just when we'd got the cordial business really rolling. He had cancer and wrote that he couldn't face the pain. I didn't even know. He just went and shot himself.'

She paused at the top of the staircase and gave his arm a sympathetic squeeze. 'That must have been dreadful for you.'

'Made me work harder. I probably owe a lot of my success to my father's death,' he said wryly, then nodded to one side of the hallway. 'Mrs Beatty's quarters are that way.' He took Kate's arm and led her in the opposite direction, opening doors as they came to them. 'Three guest-rooms . . . or children's rooms . . . and this is the master suite, bedroom, two dressing-rooms and bathroom.'

The bedroom was huge, light and airy. French doors opened on to a wide balcony which overlooked the harbour and the white and aqua furnishings delighted Kate's eye. The bathroom

was sheer luxury with its gold taps, sunken bath
and thickly carpeted floor. The cupboard-doors
in her dressing-room were mirrored and Kate
wrinkled her nose at her many-reflected images.

'I'm not sure I could stand this early in the
morning. I shall have to shut my eyes.'

'Change anything you don't like.'

'Oh, I didn't mean . . .'

He cut off her protest. 'This is your home,
Kate. Please yourself.'

'Thank you, Alex. That's very generous of
you.'

He smiled. 'You don't ask for much, Mary
Kathleen. Come on. I'll show you the formal
rooms and see what you think of them.'

There was a cynical edge to that last comment
which stirred Kate's curiosity. Leading from the
foyer, Alex showed her his study and the
breakfast-room, pointed to the kitchen and the
laundry, then led her into the formal lounge.

A marble fire-place held pride of place. Two
elegant sofas upholstered in rose-pink velvet were
set on either side of a marble and gilt coffee-
table. Tapestried armchairs provided supple-
mentary seating but the sofas dominated the
furnishings. The dove-grey carpet made no
impact. Neither did the white curtains on the
windows. The highly polished rosewood cabinets
looked decorative but strangely unused, as if they
were only for show. The wallpaper was a faintly
pink, watered silk and there were no paintings on
the wall, only a huge, gilt-edged mirror above the
fire-place.

An archway led to the dining-room which was
equally spacious. Ten chairs in the same pink

velvet were set around a table of black Venetian glass. The chandelier above the table was magnificent, as was the rosewood sideboard. The rooms had a clinical beauty, an interior decorator's beauty, but Kate felt they lacked warmth and personality despite the money which had obviously been expended lavishly. They looked like a stage-set, not part of a real home.

Alex was observing her with keen interest. 'Well?'

'It's all very elegant, Alex.'

'But?'

She shrugged. 'They're a bit too much like show-pieces if you know what I mean. Not for living in.'

He chuckled but there was little amusement in the sound. 'Oh, I do. Indeed I do know exactly what you mean. Show-piece is precisely the word,' he said derisively. 'I give you free rein to throw the lot out and start again. You'll never be comfortable with that pink anyway. It clashes with your hair.'

'Yes, it does rather,' she agreed with a grimace.

He grinned and held out a hand to her. 'Come. I'll take you downstairs. You'll like the garden-room.'

He was right. The lower level of the house was divided in half. One one side of a bar and snack area was a billiards room. The other side was a magnificent conservatory, glassed on three sides, and where it protruded from the main building to enclose an inground swimming pool, the roof was also of glass. Ferns abounded everywhere, hanging baskets, huge flower-urns and a bark garden running the length of one wall. Cane furniture with gaily printed cushions provided all the comfort one could wish.

Alex draw out a chair for her to sit down at a table. From its position she had a sweeping view of the harbour and Kate gazed out over the dazzling water to the yacht which rode at anchor. It was only two months since she and Scott had hurried past this house, down the sandstone steps to the jetty below. It seemed strange to be sitting here now as Alex's wife and mistress of his home.

'It's a beautiful room, Alex,' she sighed.

'Why the sigh?'

She flashed him an ironic smile. 'How quickly my life has changed!'

An irritable frown creased his forehead. 'Forget the past.'

Voices raised in terse disagreement drew their attention to the stairs.

'Don't be ridiculous, Mrs Beatty. I know they're home and I don't intend to be fobbed off.'

'Mrs Pallister, if you'll please . . .'

'Where is he? Upstairs or down?'

'Please wait in here and I'll inform Mr Dalton . . .'

The words became indistinct and Kate glanced quickly at Alex, surprising a gleam of malicious satisfaction in his eyes. He smiled and the smile held a predatory anticipation.

'It seems my mother couldn't wait for an invitation to meet you.' The housekeeper appeared at the head of the stairs and he called out, 'You'd better make that coffee for three, Mrs Beatty. Apparently my mother is joining us.'

'Very well, Mr Dalton. I'll tell Mrs Pallister you're here,' the housekeeper replied with cool formality.

'They don't like each other,' Alex murmured.

Kate had already surmised that. She took a deep breath and mentally prepared herself for a confrontation of some sort. The vibrations coming from Alex did not belong to a normal mother-and-son relationship and he had given her fair warning that his mother was unlikely to welcome her as a daughter-in-law. It was on the tip of her tongue to ask Alex if she looked presentable but she caught back the words, determined not to care what his mother thought of her.

When their visitor appeared Kate was almost disarmed by the pleasant smile directed at them both. It did not waver one millimetre as she walked down the stairs, making her entrance with all the panache of a seasoned performer.

CHAPTER NINE

ALEX'S mother did not even look fifty let alone the minimum sixty years she had to admit by virtue of her son's existence. Her champagne-blonde hair was stylishly groomed in a short, fluffy arrangement which softened the reality of skin tightly stretched across high cheekbones. Kate suspected that a face-lift had helped create the illusion of youth. A subtle, pastel make-up and the smartly tailored trouser suit completed the effect. She was almost as tall as Alex, fashionably slim, and she moved with all the conscious grace of a woman who was used to and expected admiration.

'Well, Alex,' she said with a silky lilt. 'I'm sure you're pleased with succeeding in your passion for privacy, but will you now kindly introduce me to your wife?' One beautifully manicured hand was extended to Kate and the smile became more brilliant. 'My dear, you must have wondered what Alex was hiding from you. Let me assure you that I and his friends are civilised human beings, although there are some doubts about your husband,' she added with an arch look at her son.

'Kate, my mother, Vera Pallister.'

'Such an off-hand introduction,' his mother reproved mockingly.

'I'm pleased to meet you, Mrs Pallister,' Kate smiled, not to be outdone in civility.

'Oh, do call me Vera. We can't be formal now that we're legally related.' She took the chair Alex held out for her. 'Thank you, dear. You have everyone completely agog at the news of your marriage but I assume that was your intention.'

Alex sat down again, tilting his chair back as he stretched out his legs and thrust his hands in his pockets. 'Don't assume too much, Mother. It's always a mistake,' he replied carelessly.

'When one is given no information, the only course left is to assume.'

'Your opening statement said it all. I have a passion for privacy.'

Vera Pallister sighed in mock exasperation as she turned to Kate. 'He's impossible. Why did you marry him?'

The question was flippantly put but the blue eyes were razor-sharp.

'I thought he'd make a good father for the children I hope to have,' Kate answered lightly and was rewarded by an approving grin from Alex.

'Have you known each other long?' Vera's hands fluttered prettily. 'It's so incredible that you managed to keep your relationship such a secret. But, of course, you were married until very recently, weren't you, dear? Such a tragic accident, your husband's death, and so awkward for you, its happening off Alex's yacht.'

The venom was coated with sweet sympathy but the poisonous darts hit Kate hard. The sheer unexpectedness of the attack robbed her of words. Alex slid smoothly to the rescue.

'I didn't find it awkward at all, Mother. Scott's death was very convenient. It meant that I didn't have to wait for Kate to divorce him. Not like Pallister. But then Pallister didn't have to wait, did he? You were all too willing to live with him.' He paused for the barb to sink home then added, 'Kate, now, is a woman of unusually high principles in today's society. She wouldn't even consider becoming my mistress, despite the usually successful inducements.'

'A woman in love doesn't stop to think of principles, Alex,' his mother retorted curtly.

'Oh, really? How kind of you to enlighten me! The strange reasoning of a woman's mind has always puzzled me. Kate is refreshingly straightforward. I know exactly where I stand with her.'

'I see. So it was marriage or nothing, Alex,' his mother said with sly condescension.

'On the contrary. My intention was always marriage. I proposed to Kate on the third day of our acquaintance. Isn't that right, darling?'

The uncharacteristic endearment surprised Kate but she had recovered enough to come in on cue. 'Yes. He was most persistent.'

'Well, having found the woman I wanted for my wife I wasn't about to let you go, my love.'

He was enjoying himself, relishing the confusion he was creating in his mother's mind. Vera Pallister looked at Kate as if trying to discern what had attracted her son so strongly. Mrs Beatty suddenly appeared and stomped downstairs. She moved straight to the bar area and slid open a door to a dumb waiter. Without a word she carried over a loaded tray and set refreshments out on the table.

'Thank you, Mrs Beatty. That's fine,' Alex declared cheerfully.

The housekeeper nodded and headed back upstairs.

'Kate?'

She hurriedly took up the coffee-pot and played the role of hostess while Alex sat with a faintly smug expression on his face.

'I've arranged a belated wedding reception for you on Saturday night. A reception, not a formal dinner. It will give Kate an opportunity to meet everyone who matters,' Vera declared as if bestowing a great favour.

Kate's hackles had been rising ever since the reference to Scott's death. She was now fighting fit. 'That was a kind thought, Vera, and very generous of you. I'm curious to meet the people whom you think matter, but I can't guarantee they will matter to me, so please don't make any more arrangements on my account. I'm sure Alex will see that I meet whomever he wishes me to meet.'

Alex laughed, a joyous ripple of sound. 'What a wife!' he spluttered triumphantly. 'You see, Mother, Kate has the exceptionally good judgment to realise that her husband is the only person who matters. Extraordinary in this day and age, isn't it? Do you wonder that I adore her?'

'You adoration seems to have a short life-span, Alex,' his mother retorted sceptically. 'I've had Nicole weeping on my shoulder.'

'Tears of vexation, no doubt.'

'You did jilt her.'

'Jilt? Jilt, Mother? What a delightfully old-fashioned word! You surprise me with such vocabulary. As I recall, jilt means to lead one on falsely then throw one over for another. Despite your wide experience you can only be applying that word to me out of ignorance.'

Alex's voice still retained its tone of light amusement but Kate noted that his eyes had narrowed to mere slits. The lazy-lidded pose hid his real thoughts.

'You let her redecorate the house.'

'Nicole is supposed to be a talented interior decorator and she was paid for her professional services. I thought the fee exorbitant and the result . . . the result was an eye-opener,' he added derisively.

'Everyone thought . . .'

'Then everyone was wrong,' Alex cut her off impatiently. 'Enough of Nicole. You're in the company of my wife. My wife,' he repeated emphatically. 'Please remember that. I'm an even-tempered man, a reasonably tolerant man, but a very bad enemy. You do understand, don't you, Mother? Thank you for arranging a reception. I'm sure you wanted to publicly welcome Kate as your daughter-in-law but we'll have no speeches or ceremony. Just a casual, friendly night. Agreed?'

'I'll never understand you, Alex.' She stood up and looked down at him disdainfully. 'But I suppose I'll have to gloss over your eccentricity.'

'Discretion is an admirable quality, and I do admire you, Mother,' Alex smiled sardonically. 'You have style.'

Vera cast a look of irony towards Kate. 'I hope you have style, my dear. You're undoubtedly clever but you're going to need style. Saturday night should be very interesting. Nine o'clock,

Alex. You can make an entrance with your bride.'
She smiled and bestowed a gracious nod on Kate
as she turned away.

'Oh, by the way, make the Champagne Veuve
Cliquot. I know you prefer Dom Perignon but we
are your star guests,' Alex drawled.

'Thank you for the reminder, Alex. I wouldn't
care to displease you and your taste does change
so rapidly,' Vera tossed over her shoulder, not
pausing in her step.

'Always for the better, Mother.'

His dry retort went unchallenged. Kate
suspected that Vera Pallister could not readily
find a line to top it. Her exit had all the stately
dignity of a queen.

And a queen she was in her own limited world.
Kate had not initially connected Alex's mother
with the Vera Pallister of the social pages but the
image fitted too well for it to be a mistake.
Newspapers and women's magazines frequently
reported the doings of Vera Pallister. She was the
organiser of charity balls and star-studded
premières, an acclaimed hostess in Sydney
society, as formidable a personality as Alex in her
own way.

The relationship between mother and son was
too complex to be easily unravelled but it was
clear that they had at least a grudging respect for
each other. They actually enjoyed the clash of
wits, probing and fencing with long-practised
skill. Apparently Alex had bitterly condemned
Vera for deserting him and his father but he had
not disowned her. The bond of blood was too
strong. She was his mother, however much he
criticised her values.

'No comment, Kate?' he asked mockingly.

'It's none of my business.'

He cocked a quizzical eyebrow at her. 'You really don't give a damn, do you?'

'What she thinks of me? No.'

'She liked that, you know. You surprised her.' He gave a soft chuckle. 'She doesn't know what to think.'

'Which was your intention . . . darling.'

This time it was a full-blooded laugh. He threw back his head and let it bubble out uninhibitedly. Finally he stood up and rounded the table. He pulled her up into a loose embrace. 'Perhaps I think you are a darling,' he smiled.

'Next you'll be telling me I'm your love,' she scoffed.

His smile drained away. One hand came up and gripped her chin as his eyes held hers with hard intensity. 'You're more important to me than any other woman. I need you, Mary Kathleen.'

His kiss was hard, demanding, uncharacteristic of his usual lovemaking. She sensed a slip in his control and even as she responded she wondered what had triggered it.

'God, how I need that sweetness!' he muttered. 'Now. Come to bed with me now.'

He took her compliance for granted and hurried her up the stairs, not pausing until they were inside their bedroom with the door shut behind them. Then he swung her hard against him and kissed her with hungry passion. He walked her backwards to the bed, his mouth still devouring hers. Then he was stripping them both with swift efficiency, carrying her with him to lie full-length in the closest intimacy.

There were no preliminary caresses but his strange wildness had excited her and she was ready for his urgent thrust for possession. Their union was an insatiable cry for all else to be blotted out until the only reality was the feverish pounding of hearts yearning to become one. Time stretched on but they were only aware of fulfilling their needs, tuning and retuning their bodies to one pagan song after another in a long paean of savage sensuality. When exhaustion finally claimed them they lay in a silence throbbing with unspoken thoughts.

Kate felt completely ravished, body and soul. All her defences had disintegrated and she knew if Alex asked anything of her at this moment she would give it to him. She wished that he loved her and the wish brought a wave of deep sadness. Tears started to her eyes and she lifted a hand to dash them away.

'Kate?'

The lump in her throat made it impossible to answer the soft query. She closed her eyes and turned her head into the pillow as Alex raised himself to look down at her. With gentle insistence he turned her over and there was nothing she could do to hide the revealing wetness on her cheeks.

'Oh, hell!' he groaned and cradled her gently in his arms, his mouth raining warm kisses over her hair. 'I'm sorry, Kate. I had no right to use you like that. It won't happen again, I swear it.'

'It's all right,' she choked out. 'I didn't mind.'

He pulled away and searched her eyes anxiously. 'Then why the tears?'

She managed a shaky smile. 'I was just being silly. Truly, it's all right, Alex.'

'I was savage, inconsiderate, plain, bloody selfish,' he bit out with grim distaste.

'No.' She reached up and stroked his cheek, loving him for his concern even as she accepted that he had been working out some devil inside himself. 'I liked it. I really did.'

He sighed and lay back down, pulling her across his chest and caressing her back with light fingers. 'Kate, about Saturday night. We don't have to go. It might be ... an ordeal for you. There's no obligation ...'

'I don't mind playing the part of your wife,' she assured him.

His fingers stopped and dug into the softness of her skin. 'You're not playing a part, Mary Kathleen. You are my wife.'

'I meant ... well, if you wanted to give people the impression that ... that we're in love ... I'll play along with you.'

The stroking started again. His chest rose and fell several times before he replied. 'No. I don't want you to pretend. I hate pretence.'

'You were pretending to your mother,' she pointed out.

'The trick with my mother is never to give her a weapon she can turn back on to you. Keep her guessing so she's never sure of the terrain. That way you stay ahead and can't be got at. She loves to manipulate.'

'You're alike, you know,' Kate murmured softly.

He was silent for a long time. 'No,' he finally breathed. 'To me it's a cynical game, but it's

Mother's whole way of life, one long ego-trip, flexing her power. I believe she actually did love my father but because he couldn't be manipulated into doing what she wanted, she left him for Pallister who was well positioned to let her chase her ambition. I once asked Dad why he didn't hate her. He said she couldn't help herself, that her obsession wouldn't let her be content in the roles of wife and mother.

'She barely raised a tear when Pallister died but when Dad shot himself she completely broke up. I was staggered. Her grief was undeniably genuine. Up until then I'd hated her, refused to have anything to do with her. I still despise her scale of values but . . . maybe Dad was right. She couldn't help herself. And I've come to appreciate her own particular charisma.'

While he was still in the mood to confide such personal details to her, Kate decided to press the one question which was all-important. 'Alex, will you give me a straight answer if I ask something?'

'Depends on what it is.' He twined her hair around his fingers and gave it a gentle tug. 'You keep your innermost thoughts secret, Kate. Allow me the same privacy.'

She propped herself up and saw the guarded expression on his face. 'Well, I'll ask anyway. You don't have to answer. Why didn't you marry Nicole?'

A spark of hatred flickered briefly and was gone. His mouth took on an ugly, sardonic twist. 'You've seen her handiwork. When you see Nicole you'll realise that our formal rooms downstairs are the perfect setting for her. A setting, Kate. What does that tell you?'

'That she wants to be a star?'

'Like my mother. Marriage to me was her launching-pad. I didn't want a wife like my mother. I wanted a wife like you, a wife who wants children and is content to make a family, a wife who gives her husband loyalty no matter how much of a bastard he is. Scott was a fool, wasting his time on tinsel, too blind to see the gold he was trampling underfoot.' His eyes softened as he smiled her. 'But I recognised your value, Mary Kathleen. Persuading you to marry me was the best day's work I've ever done.'

But you love Nicole Fouvet. The thought slid into Kate's mind and she knew intuitively that it was true. Alex had called love a messy emotion which could not guarantee happiness and his will was strong enough to overrule his heart. He had rejected Nicole and married Kate in a coldly calculated decision. But today his mother had forced the image of Nicole back into his mind and he had needed to wipe it out. That accounted for the prolonged ferocity of his lovemaking.

She understood a great deal now, the ruthless speed with which he had carried through his decision, the determination to make their relationship work well. He had been compelled to prove himself right, that marriage to Kate was better than the marriage he could have had with Nicole.

Kate crushed the instinctive impulse to crawl back into her protective shell. She lay down again and knew before her head hit the pillow that she was going to fight. She suddenly recognised how negative and defeatist her attitude had been, letting fear rule her life and limiting herself to what was safe. Her marriage was not safe as long as Alex still loved Nicole Fouvet and Kate could no longer pretend that her emotions were not involved. They were very much involved and she was not going to be passive any more.

She liked what she had with Alex and no one was going to take it from her, not Nicole, his mother or anyone else. She would fight with every weapon at her disposal and even if she could not win his love, she would do her utmost to prevent his ever straying from her side. Alex was her husband and the father . . .

'You've gone very quiet. What are you thinking?'

'I think I might be pregnant.'

That wiped Nicole Fouvet out of his mind, Kate thought with sharp satisfaction. Alex's reaction was all she could want. He leaned over her, his eyes shining with joy and a huge grin on his face.

'That's great! That's fantastic!'

She smiled, happy that his excitement matched hers. 'It's probably too soon to be absolutely sure. I'll go to a doctor for a check-up next week.'

'The first of our ten,' he said smugly.

Laughter swelled up in her and bubbled out of her throat.

'Don't you want ten?' he demanded with mock disappointment.

She stroked his cheek. 'If that's what you want, that's what we'll have.'

He bent down and kissed her, reverently, with a lingering sweetness which curled around Kate's heart.

'You'll make a beautiful mother,' he whispered huskily.

It was the first time Kate had heard deep emotion in his voice. His desire for children was as great as her own and the knowledge gave her some peace of mind because this was her ultimate power. She could give him his children.

Looking back now on her marriage to Scott, Kate knew that she had never really loved her first husband. Her feeling had been more of a giddy intoxication that this wonderfully handsome man had singled her out. She had been so proud of him, his looks and his charm. Being with him had made her feel like a princess. But Scott had had the heart and mind of a frog and the spell of romance had worn thin with their living together.

Living with Alex had been an entirely different experience. The more she was with him, the more she had come to appreciate the man he was. Her love for him was no superficial attraction. It was the inner core of him which warmed her soul; his kindness and understanding, patience and generosity. He answered her needs.

The question was, could she answer his? His need for children, yes, and she was reasonably sure he was sexually satisfied. In most other areas Alex seemed self-sufficient, but there had to be something that Nicole Fouvet supplied which Kate didn't. Was it style? The type of style and charisma Alex admired in his mother? Was that what attracted him, even against his will?

It was no use taxing her mind about it now. Nothing was more certain than the certainty that Nicole Fouvet would form part of Vera Pallister's reception on Saturday night. Alex's reaction to her should shed some light on the threat she posed to the happiness Kate hoped for. In the meantime Alex was here and she would do her best to please him. Whatever Saturday night brought, Kate would meet it head on. There would be no backward steps in this marriage.

CHAPTER TEN

'WEAR the white dress, Kate.'

She was blow-drying her hair into a fluffy mass of waves. Alex preferred it unconfined and tonight she was intent on pleasing him. 'You're sure?' she asked uncertainly. 'I thought the violet one had more . . .'

'No. The white,' he said decisively.

'You actually want me to look like a bride?'

'I like you in white. It's the best foil for your hair.'

He had answered matter-of-factly but Kate sensed the thread of tension in him. He did not normally concern himself with her apparel so her appearance tonight held some importance to him. The thought teased Kate's mind as she applied a soft make-up with meticulous care. She needed colour in her face if she was wearing white but too much colour would look harsh.

The dress he had chosen was very feminine. Long, flowing sleeves were gathered into gold-embroidered bands at her wrist. The V-neckline was daringly low, dropping almost to her waist which was accentuated by a wide gold belt. A band of gold embroidery encircled the hem of the skirt, adding glamour to its soft folds. Kate slipped her feet into the elegant gold sandals Alex had bought her then examined her appearance critically in the mirrored doors of her dressing-room.

Her throat looked too bare with such a low décolletage. She rummaged in her jewellery-box, tried some gold chains and a string of cultured pearls but nothing looked right. She frowned, not liking the bare effect but unable to correct it. She hurried into the bedroom.

'I can't wear this dress, Alex. It needs a necklace and I haven't anything suitable.'

He looked up from straightening a cuff-link and smiled. 'You have now. Come here.'

He was standing in front of the feature dressing-table and as she walked forward he turned and opened a large velvet box.

'Stand still,' he instructed casually.

She gasped as he slid the necklace around her throat. The narrow gold band curved down into a sharp V from which hung a huge tear-drop pearl, encircled with diamonds and set in gold.

'Like it?'

'It's absolutely beautiful. Thank you, Alex.'

'I'll let you put the earrings on. I haven't the expertise.'

'Is this why you wanted me to wear this dress?' she asked, pleasure sparkling in her eyes.

'One of the reasons. You look lovely, Kate. Just how I wanted you to look. You'll stand out like a shaft of light in that crowd.' His fingers caressed the line of her throat and raked softly through the cloud of red-gold hair. 'A fiery angel, an intriguing mixture of purity and seductiveness. One look at you and curiosity will be satisfied.' Cynicism curved his mouth. 'Stupid, isn't it? But effective.'

'I'm on show,' she said flatly, her joy in the gift fizzling out.

'You know you are.'

'Yes, I know.'

She veiled her disappointment with lowered lashes but he tilted her chin up questioningly.

'You said it didn't worry you.'

'It doesn't worry me,' she retorted sharply. 'It worries you.'

His hand dropped to her shoulder and he squeezed it unconsciously. 'You're wrong,' he asserted in a tightly restrained voice.

'Am I?' She lifted her head higher and challenged him. 'The game might not be all-important to you, Alex, but you want it played your way. This dress and the jewellery are just props, aren't they? You didn't buy them for my pleasure. You're simply setting me up to prove something tonight.'

He frowned. 'They were bought for your protection.'

'No, for your pride. I don't need protection. Don't pretend to me, Alex. Like you, I hate pretence.'

She stepped around him and snatched up the earrings from the velvet case. Her hands were trembling slightly but she managed to fasten them on with a semblance of composure. Alex stood behind her. She knew he was watching her in the mirror but she did not meet his eyes.

He looked very impressive in formal clothes, handsome in a mature, distinguished way. With a heavy heart Kate wondered how many women tonight would be coveting her the man she had married. Certainly Nicole Fouvet. She was the dangerous threat. She was almost certainly the reason for Alex's interest in Kate's appearance. It made Kate feel sick with apprehension but she was determined not to be intimidated by the woman, however beautiful she was.

'There!' she sighed, fluffing her hair out so that the earrings were visible. 'I hope you're satisfied with your investment.'

'Kate . . .' There was a pained look in his eyes, a grim set to his mouth. He made an indecisive gesture, half apology, half protest, then turned away. 'Change into whatever you like. I don't care. I married the person, not the finery.'

Remember that, Alex, she silently commanded as she reached out and plucked at his sleeve. He glanced back at her, his face tightly shuttered.

'I'm sorry for being prickly. I do want to please you, Alex,' she said softly.

He sighed and gathered her into a warm embrace. His lips brushed across her hair. 'You please me, Mary Kathleen. Very much.'

And hold on to that thought too, she willed, intent on building as many safeguards as she could against the attraction of Nicole Fouvet.

'If you'd prefer not to go tonight . . .'

She smiled up at him. 'And give your mother ammunition against me? Never.'

She won a smile from him even if it was a wry one. 'Sure you don't mind?'

'Of course not,' she insisted but let her mouth droop a little. 'I just got the impression that . . . you needed to justify your choice of wife. I was a show-piece for Scott. I didn't like the idea that . . .'

He pressed a finger to her lips and his eyes were hard with determination. 'I don't want a show-piece and I couldn't have chosen a better wife.'

A flare of triumph warmed her veins. She was ready to face Nicole Fouvet now. 'Thank you, Alex. I couldn't have chosen a better husband. I only have to fetch my evening-bag and we can go.'

Mrs Beatty was loitering in the foyer and she beamed up at them as they walked downstairs. 'My, you do look an impressive couple.' The weather-beaten face flushed red with embarrassment. 'I didn't say it before but I'll say it now. I'm so happy for you both that you found each other.'

'I'm glad you approve, Mrs Beatty,' Alex said lightly. 'We can surely look forward to domestic bliss.'

'Oh, Mr Dalton, it's not up to me to approve or disapprove, but I'm sure you couldn't have married a nicer girl.' She made a fuss of opening the front door for them. 'I hope you have a lovely night out.'

Touched by the housekeeper's warmth, Kate leaned forward and kissed her on the cheek. 'Good night, Mrs Beatty, and thank you.'

The older woman clucked with pleasure and waved them out.

'You've won a heart,' Alex murmured sardonically as he led Kate into the garage.

'It's a very kind heart,' she answered seriously. 'Do you know she sends almost all her wages to her daughter? The poor thing is a deserted wife with three little kids.'

'She told you that?'

'It slipped out in conversation while I was cooking dinner last night.'

'You don't have to cook, you know.'

'I wanted to and Mrs Beatty didn't mind.'

'I'm sure she didn't,' he said with a short laugh. 'And neither did I,' he added warmly as he opened the passenger door of the Lamborghini.

Kate paused and looked up at him. 'I'm happy to be able to do something for you, Alex. You've been so very generous to me.'

She stepped into the car and had settled herself comfortably with the seat-belt fastened before Alex shut the door. He took his own seat in silence and did not attempt any conversation during the drive to his mother's residence. Kate hoped she had supplied him with food for thought. She wanted the advantages in their marriage at the forefront of his mind when the inevitable confrontation with Nicole occurred.

Vera's home was situated in a fashionable area of French's Forest. A high wall ensured the privacy of the extensive block of land. The house itself was an impressive brick edifice with white Grecian colonnades. Style, Kate thought grimly and tilted her chin a little higher as Alex pressed the doorbell.

The door was opened by Vera herself, resplendent in a chiffon caftan which floated around her in shades of peach and apricot. Her smile was all graciousness with only a dash of smug delight. 'My dear Kate, what a clever choice of dress! Yours or Alex's?'

'Alex's of course,' Kate replied airily as if the question was irrelevant.

'Of course,' Vera echoed, a little nonplussed by Kate's manner but recovering quickly. 'Punctual as always, Alex.'

'A matter of courtesy, Mother,' he answered dryly. 'Shall we go in?'

'Impatient to see someone?'

'No. Just thirsty.'

'I have the Veuve Cliquot all ready on ice.'

'The perfect hostess . . . as always.'

The buzz of conversation immediately dropped as Vera led them into what could only be called a reception room. The parquet floor was polished to a high gleam. Ceiling-tall mirrors separated several sets of French doors around the walls and elaborate floral arrangements were placed with a sure professional touch for maximum effect. As befitting such a room the people in it were expensively dressed and groomed to slick perfection. They stood in companionable groups, leaving a clear central space and Kate had the impression that this had been stage-managed to focus attention on her and Alex.

Vera had detailed a waiter to be on hand near the entrance. His tray carried a silver ice-bucket containing Alex's choice of champagne and Vera insisted on pouring them each a glass, thus keeping all three of them poised there, very much in the spotlight. Kate kept her attention on Vera who was suddenly full of light banter.

'Quite a gathering for such short notice, Mother,' Alex commented sardonically.

'The evening does have its points of interest.'

Vera's gaze challenged her son mockingly then flicked towards the far end of the room. A heightened expectancy seemed to ripple through the crowd of guests. Eyes darted back and forth, then focused avidly on the one woman whose back was still turned to them. Her companion touched her arm and gave a nod. She slowly swung around and Kate had no trouble guessing her identity.

Nicole Fouvet was breathtakingly beautiful. And knew it. The exquisite perfection of her face commanded admiration even before the superb body whose generous curves were displayed with sophisticated chic. Her pale olive skin was offset by raven-black hair which had been severely styled into a snood effect at the back of her head. Around her long, graceful neck was a black ribbon supporting a pink taffeta rose under one ear. Her gown was of black taffeta. Its stiffly frilled collar framed her face then curved past the swell of voluptuous breasts to a nipped in waistline where a wide sash was lined with the same pink as the rose. She looked magnificent.

After a moment's pause she began walking down the room towards them. She moved like royalty, slowly, gracefully, very much assured of her star quality. If Vera Pallister was the queen of Sydney society, then here, for all intents and purposes, was the crown princess. This was Vera's challenge to Kate as well as to Alex, testing the supposed indifference of her son to Nicole and the mettle of her new daughter-in-law.

Kate took a firm grip on herself, determined to counter the attack which was coming. Nicole smiled but the smile was only directed at Alex. Kate steeled herself not to look at him, not to reveal any concern about his reaction.

Nicole lifted her hand and purred in a soft, husky voice, 'Alex, how lovely to see you.'

For one awful second Kate thought he was

going to kiss the hand offered but he merely pressed it lightly and let it go.

'It's always a pleasure to see you, Nicole,' he said smoothly. 'Kate, may I introduce Nicole Fouvet. Nicole, my wife.'

Nicole's remarkable aquamarine eyes moved reluctantly to Kate and their feline depths nursed a gleam of hostility. Kate smiled broadly. Vera Pallister had taught her how to disarm people.

'It seems absurd to say how do you do when you obviously do everything so well, and I agree with my husband that it must always be a pleasure to see you. You're so very beautiful, Nicole.'

'Thank you,' Nicole replied, unable to hide a startled flicker. 'How very direct you are!'

'Kate is nothing if not direct. Wouldn't you agree, Mother?'

Kate was relieved to hear the dry note of amusement in his voice.

'Yes. Very direct,' Vera murmured, eyeing Kate thoughtfully.

Ignoring Kate's presence and confident of her power, Nicole wound her arm around Alex's and looked up at him with blatant invitation. 'Well, I'm glad you're home again, darling. I've missed you. I won't let you go again.'

Kate laughed and her subsequent smile held an equally blatant indulgence. 'You must feel terribly flattered, Alex. It'd be a pity not to enjoy such fulsome attention. Would you like to stay with Nicole while your mother introduces me around?'

'Don't you wish me to accompany you, Kate?' he replied in an ominously quiet tone.

'You know I don't require you to do anything you don't want to do, Alex,' she answered blithely. 'Make your own choice.'

Kate held her breath but the challenge worked for her. Alex disengaged himself from the clinging hand.

'Please excuse me, Nicole. I'm sure you won't lack company.'

'Perhaps we'll see you later, Nicole,' Kate added graciously.

'I'll make a point of it,' Nicole said with venomous sweetness.

Round one to the wife, Kate exulted as she saw a measure of grudging respect in Vera's eyes and felt Alex's arm slide around her waist. He drew her over to the closest group of people and the introductions began. Vera saw that they circulated from group to group, obviously monitoring how well Kate was being received by her guests. They drank only champagne. Waiters offered trays of delicacies from time to time and Kate kept eating them to settle her nervous stomach. She estimated that there were some eighty guests and she met and smiled at every one of them, answering questions with the confidence of a woman who had her husband's love.

Alex good-humouredly played his part but there was no real rapport between them. He had closed in upon himself and Kate could only sense an inner stillness as if he was waiting for something. Occasionally she caught him observing her with an odd look of speculation but most of his attention was claimed by friends and acquaintances.

Kate's facial muscles began to ache. Her inner tension was hard to contain and the strain of appearing relaxed and confident was slowly taking its toll. Vera had virtually pushed Sir Edward Mills on to them and the old politician was being long-winded in his mission to interest Alex in giving up private enterprise and turning his talents to public service.

'We need men like you in parliament. I'll be retiring before the next election and I'd like to nominate you for my seat. A married man should settle down and be responsible. Isn't that right, my dear?'

His eyes twinkled at Kate and she smiled stiffly as he tweaked the white, pork-chop whiskers which obviously compensated him for his bald pate. Alex seemed interested so she took the opportunity to excuse herself from the conversation which looked like continuing for some time. A brief visit to the powder room would give her a much-needed breathing space.

Careful not to catch anyone's eye, Kate weaved around groups of people and hurried down a hallway which had been pointed out to her by Vera some time previously. The first door she came to led into a bedroom. The light was on and Kate slipped inside and closed the door behind her. This was as good a place as any to be alone for a while. She sat down at the dressing-table and lightly rubbed her temples, trying to hold back the headache which was threatening. On the whole she thought she had handled the evening reasonably well. Nicole had not come near them again and perhaps she saw now that Alex was no longer vulnerable to her charms. Kate hoped that was true but she doubted it. There was too much evidence to the contrary.

The door clicked open and she glanced around to see Nicole Fouvet entering the room. She closed the door and stood with her back against it in a haughty pose, surveying Kate with malicious satisfaction.

'How clever of you to find a private place for our conversation,' she began with silky sarcasm. 'But then you are clever. You must have been in exactly the right place at the right time to have got Alex to the altar. Would you like to tell me how you managed it?'

'You omitted one important phrase. I was also the right person,' Kate retorted pointedly. Then affecting an air of complete unconcern she opened her evening-bag, took out a comb and began running it through her hair. 'As for managing anything, I leave that to Alex. He's so very efficient.'

'He only married you to get back at me,' Nicole stated with barely repressed anger.

Kate stopped combing and raised a quizzical eyebrow. 'Do you think so? How self-centred of you.'

'I know it.' Her voice rang with absolute conviction. With supreme confidence she walked over and took up a position behind Kate so that her face was reflected above Kate's in the mirror. 'Do you imagine he could possibly prefer you to me?' she demanded haughtily, 'Alex loves me, and even you must see that I'm the woman who belongs at his side. He married you in a fit of pique but now that he's back in circulation, he won't be able to keep away from me.'

'Oh, I think he can resist your so obvious charms, Nicole,' Kate drawled derisively. 'He managed to tonight.'

Contempt flashed into the aquamarine eyes. 'You might get Alex to play the dutiful husband for a while, but once you give him what he wants, don't expect to keep him. He only married you to have his precious children.'

That was a punch below the belt but Kate gave no indication of the pain it caused. She forced out a smile of sweet condescension. 'Well, if that's what you think, Nicole, perhaps it's only a kindness to tell you that Alex and I plan on having ten children. He has a fancy to be captain of his own cricket team. I really wouldn't wait around that long if I were you. It'd be a terrible waste of all that stunning beauty. Much more profitable for you to find a husband you can control, as Vera did.'

'You bitch! You only married him for a meal-ticket.'

The claws were bared with a vengeance. This was no longer hostility but sheer hatred and bitter enmity. Kate stared back at her rival with icy eyes and her words were coldly deliberate, each one a biting thrust.

'Let this be clear to you, Nicole. I will remain Alex's wife. I will take my rightful place at his side in any public social gathering and I shall not be embarrassed by any scene you care to create. If your ambition is to play second string to me, then by all means, pursue my husband, but I'll never let him go and you cannot intimidate me into giving up my position.'

'You'll only make a fool of yourself trying to

cling on to him,' Nicole snarled. 'And as for your ten children, you'll be lucky to conceive one. He'll be sharing my bed, not yours.'

'What a crude woman you are underneath that polish!' Kate replied disdainfully.

An angry flush stained Nicole's cheeks and fury stabbed out at Kate. 'I'll get what I want you smug little chit. And tonight is not yet over.'

Having hurled down the gauntlet Nicole made a swift exit. Kate sagged with relief. Round two had been a stand-off, she decided, but was unable to stem the wave of depression which rolled over her. They had been brave words she had flung at Nicole, fighting words, but Kate knew she did not have the stomach to carry through on them. If Alex broke his word and was unfaithful to her she would curl up and die.

The bitter truth was that Alex had never pretended anything else but that children was his motive for marrying her. That was their bond. There had been no obligation for him to reveal his past relationship with Nicole but he had promised fidelity in their marriage contract. Kate could not, would not share her husband with another woman. Never again. It was too much to ask of love to suffer through that humiliation.

Suddenly Nicole's last words hammered on her brain. The night was not yet over. She had to return to the party. Stay at Alex's side. With a flutter of panic Kate picked up her comb and bag and hurried out.

CHAPTER ELEVEN

'Ah, there you are, my dear.' Vera moved smoothly into action as soon as Kate re-entered the reception room, She linked arms and proceeded at a slow stroll, drawing Kate along with her and projecting the picture of a private little *tête-à-tête* so that no one would interrupt them. 'I've been looking forward to a private chat with you. It's obviously to my advantage to get to know you better,' she declared with as much directness as Kate had given her.

'Not now, Vera,' Kate said abruptly, her eyes darting around the room in search of Alex. He was not in the corner where she had left him, although he might have tired of standing and sat down somewhere. There were too many guests milling around, obscuring her view. 'Is Alex still with Sir Edward?' she asked, sure that Vera would have kept tabs on her son.

'I'm sure he'll be occupied for some time. Sir Edward is a pompous old bore, but a useful one. What is your attitude towards politics, Kate?'

'Negative, but naturally I shall respect Alex's wishes. He's entitled to pursue his interests. If they lie in that direction I'll give him whatever support he requires from me.'

'A very tolerant outlook. I wonder just how tolerant you are,' Vera remarked dryly and gave Kate a measuring look. 'You're a strange girl.'

'Not a girl, Vera. I've been in the adult world

for quite some time now,' Kate replied with heavy irony. 'And as for strangeness, perhaps I think you're a strange mother.'

'Some women simply aren't cut out for motherhood. Dirty nappies have very limited appeal.'

'For a person with a limited view.'

'A matter of opinion.'

Vera's dismissive tone brought a faint smile to Kate's lips. Alex's mother did not like a conversation unless it was dictated by her. Their irreconcilable points of view made talking a waste of time as far as Kate was concerned and despite the assurance that Alex was still in Sir Edward's company, she was anxious to get back to him. Again she cast her gaze around, frowning when she could not spot either of them.

'I don't expect you to like me, Kate. Few women do. But I am a force to be reckoned with, so don't think you can ignore me.'

Kate dragged her attention back to her mother-in-law. 'I wouldn't be so rude as to ignore you, Vera, but don't expect me to kow-tow to you. I'm not entering your force-field.'

Vera raised a sceptical eyebrow. 'If you remain Alex's wife, my dear Kate, you will inevitably be drawn into it.'

'I somehow doubt that,' Kate said shortly, resenting the sly innuendo.

'Doubt that you'll remain Alex's wife?'

It took considerable effort to control her temper. The confrontation with Nicole had worn her reserves thin. Kate stopped dead and looked her contempt at Vera. 'Were you satisfied with the outcome of your opening gambit tonight, Vera?'

She smiled. 'I found it most interesting. Not what I expected, but most interesting. A tactical victory for you, my dear, but I wonder if you can keep it up. Nicole is very ambitious. She doesn't take kindly to being thwarted and I very much doubt that Alex is quite as immune to her as he pretends.'

'And of course you'd prefer her as your daughter-in-law.'

One corner of Vera's mouth curled and her eyes held a tired cynicism. 'Not necessarily. Nicole is predictable and therefore slightly boring. While you and I may never be in accord about anything, I couldn't call you a bore, not yet anyway.'

A hand tweaking white, pork-chop whiskers caught Kate's eye. She stared over Vera's shoulder as Sir Edward Mills paused near the entrance of the room and beamed down at the woman accompanying him. Kate's heart stopped. Sir Edward had been out of the room. With someone else. Not talking to Alex at all. Then where was Alex? Her heart picked up its beat, thumping a painful protest to the answer which leapt into her mind.

She sucked in a quick breath, instinctively shielding her private agony from Vera. Then drawing on every ounce of pride, she looked her scorn at the woman whose game was more important than people's feelings.

'So, you even play with lies. It's a poor game when you have to cheat, Vera. Where is Alex?'

A quick glance around revealed Sir Edward Mills' telling presence but Vera's eyes held no guilt or chagrin when they returned to Kate.

They sparked with malicious life. 'I simply led you into making a false assumption. As my son observed to me the other day, one should be careful of making assumptions. Alex thought he had me outfoxed, but I'll get my answers tonight, one way or another. He's on the terrace with Nicole. The question now, dear Kate, is which move do you make?'

There were only two choices. She could pretend that she completely trusted Alex and take the attitude that his private meeting with Nicole held no significance. She wished she could believe that but could not summon the necessary blind faith.

A sick despair was growing inside her like a malignant cancer, eating into her hopes and casting an ominous shadow over the future which had looked so promising before tonight. She was unaware of the dull bleakness which had crept into her eyes.

'Dear God!' Vera breathed, and a frown marred the careful smoothness of her face. 'I hadn't even considered that you might love him.'

Kate was instantly on guard, tightening her defences and hiding behind an impassive mask. 'Do all those French doors lead on to the terrace in question?' she asked levelly, not giving anything away.

'Kate . . .' There was an uncharacteristic note of appeal in Vera's voice. She searched Kate's obdurate expression for a moment and then sighed. 'You won't believe me, but I'm sorry for the pain I've caused you tonight. If you'll take some wise advice from a woman with long years of experience, don't go out on the terrace. Leave well enough alone. You'll have Alex to yourself when you go home.'

There was a soft sincerity in the words, a sympathetic concern in her eyes. Kate was not sure if either was genuine but it did not matter. There was only one course she could take. 'You don't understand, Vera. I have to go. I'd be grateful if you'd point out the best way.'

One hand clutched Kate's arm, staying any move. 'Believe me. It's a mistake to turn it into a confrontation this time. I know Nicole and I know my son, and nothing can be gained by . . .'

'But you don't know me.' Kate brushed the hand aside. 'I'll find my own way.'

'The door at the far end of the room, near the pedestal with the sculpture.'

The words checked Kate for a moment and Vera quickly moved into step with her.

'Walk with me. If you must be a fool, at least be a discreet one. I'll cover your exit from curious eyes.'

'Why?' Kate demanded bitterly. 'You were all set to crucify me when we arrived and you've probably stage-managed getting Alex and Nicole together.'

'Yes, I arranged it. With malice aforethought,' Vera admitted wryly. She gave Kate a dry little smile as they reached the door. 'But as improbable as it sounds, I'm now on your side. You see, I did love Alex's father, and in my own twisted way I love my son. Maybe you can give him the happiness that I . . .' She broke off and shrugged. 'I could never mend the fences I smashed. I've led you to the door furthest from where they are, Kate. Don't rush in. Please reconsider before you move.'

There was nothing to reconsider. Vera might have arranged their meeting on the terrace but Alex could have walked away from Nicole. To have stayed with her for this length of time could only mean one thing. Alex was where he wanted to be. Not his promise of fidelity nor even a sense of loyalty had weighed against his inclination. Tonight of all nights he should have given Kate his full support if their marriage was to mean anything. He had broken faith with her and now she had to know how deep was the breach.

She stepped outside and shut the door with the minimum of noise. For a moment she looked back at Vera whose face suddenly looked drawn and old through the pane of glass. Someone apparently called for her attention and the practised mask of the successful hostess slipped back into place. Kate turned away.

It was a cool autumn night. The only light on the terrace was that filtering out from the reception room. Potted shrubs created long and varied shadows but the solid silhouette at the far end of the terrace held no likeness to any shrubbery.

Nicole's arms gleamed whitely against Alex's dark suit and Alex was making no move to remove them from around his neck. Kate could see one of his hands gripping Nicole's waist and she had no doubt that his other hand was similarly occupied. Nicole's perfect profile was uplifted but for the moment, Alex was talking. The deep timbre of his voice was audible but the words were too low to be distinct. They carried a note of passion.

Memories of her first marriage writhed inside

Kate like snakes of barbed wire, jabbing, tearing at the newly woven fabric of her marriage to Alex. Never again, she had vowed . . . the cheating, the lying, the thousand and one betrayals of trust, the whole degradation of living with a man who was only using you . . . never again.

She quelled the rising impulse to cringe, to turn aside and hide, to retreat and pretend she had seen nothing, heard nothing, knew nothing. Pride stiffened her spine. This time there would be no turning of the other cheek. She was no worm to slither away from a scene as if she was the guilty party. She had every right to seek out her husband.

Her high-heels clicked eerily on the tiles as she walked determinedly forward. She saw Alex's head lift abruptly, heard Nicole's sharp murmur of protest. Kate's step did not falter. She came to a halt some three metres away from them and forced her voice to sound completely disinterested.

'Pardon me for interrupting. I thought you should know that I'm going home now, Alex. Do you want to take me or shall I call a taxi?'

She heard the sharp intake of his breath. When he spoke the words were harshly clipped. 'I'll be with you in a minute, Kate. I haven't quite finished with Nicole.'

She stood perfectly still, withdrawing from him mentally and emotionally. Nicole stirred and glanced at her. The dim light picked up the malicious triumph which gleamed out of her eyes. You can have him, Nicole, Kate thought dully. He's not worth fighting for if you're what he wants.

'As you like, Alex,' she replied with cold dignity. 'I'll say goodbye to your mother. Then I intend to go, with you or without you.'

She swung on her heel and walked very carefully, one foot in front of the other, knowing each step posted the end of her marriage. She took the first door which led back inside. Even there she walked as if already completely alone, refusing recognition to the existence of people around her. Her gaze found the beacon of Vera's champagne swirl of hair and she made for it without hesitation. Before her goal was reached a hand gripped her elbow hard.

'We'll take our leave together, Kate,' Alex muttered in her ear.

He forcibly slowed her pace and they approached his mother in a leisurely fashion. He tapped Vera on the shoulder and nodded to the people grouped around her.

'Kate and I are going home now, Mother,' he announced quietly.

'But, Alex, it's so early,' she protested charmingly, but her eyes swept them both with a sharpness which held more concern then curiosity.

'You're inexhaustible. We're more human. Thank you for an enjoyable evening and good night to you all,' he said smoothly.

Vera took Kate's hand, delaying their departure. 'My dear Kate, I hope we'll be meeting again soon.' It was more a question than a statement but her probing eyes could not pierce Kate's shield.

Vera would get her answers eventually, Kate thought bitterly, and withdrew her hand. 'Good night, Vera.' It was a polite shut-out but Vera tried again.

'I'll see you out.'

'No. Please stay with your guests,' Alex insisted. 'You've been too kind already. I must repay you sometime, Mother. Good night.'

Their exit was delayed several times by friendly well-wishers but finally they were out and on their way home. Once in the car Kate lay her throbbing head back against the cold, leather seat and closed her eyes. Silence sat heavily between them until Alex made a derisive comment.

'I presume my mother sent you out on the terrace.'

That's so typical, Kate thought contemptuously. Blame anyone, your mother, your wife, your lover, anyone but yourself. Out loud she stripped him of any defence.

'You're wrong. She did not want me to look for you. In fact she tried to distract me. Only when I demanded to know where you were did she tell me, and then she did her best to persuade me to leave you alone. Leave well enough alone. It was good advice, she said. The wise, sensible, discreet thing to do. But she didn't know that I've been through it all before.' Her weary tone sharpened to bitter accusation. 'Only you know that, Alex. You knew it and disregarded it.'

'Kate . . .'

His hand felt for hers and she struck it away.

'Don't you touch me!' The command held all the vehemence of deep pain. 'At least I knew my part in your mother's game, but not in yours. Oh no! You glamourised me up and threw me to the she-wolves, knowing all their claws would be out for me. You left me in ignorance and you lied to me.'

Her voice broke on a half-sob as tears welled up in her eyes. She bit her lips hard, trying to turn back the swell of emotion which pressed against her tired defences.

'I didn't lie to you, Kate.'

You did. You did, she cried in silent agony. Tears spilled out and coursed down her cheeks. She turned her head aside and hunched her body away from him, fighting desperately to hold herself together for a little while longer, long enough to get home and shut herself away alone.

'Kate, please . . . oh, damn it all to hell!'

The powerful sports car suddenly leapt forward. The speed limit was steadily ignored right across the city but Kate made no protest. After the first abrupt acceleration she was unaware of anything but her own inner misery. When Alex finally braked the car to a halt in his garage, Kate was sluggish in stirring herself. He was out and around to her side of the car before she had even discarded her seat-belt. The door was wrenched open and his hand already at her elbow as she began to move.

'I don't need your help,' she forced out in a hoarse croak.

'Come on, Kate. Don't give me that. You think I don't know you've been crying all the way home?' he said tersely.

She swallowed in an effort to gain control of her voice. 'I can manage alone, thank you.'

He sighed and thumped the hood in frustration before stepping back and holding the door for her. Kate swung her legs out and heaved herself up, keeping the momentum going so that she was walking well ahead of Alex until she reached the front door. There she had to wait for him to unlock it. As soon as it was open she swept past him and on up the stairs. By the time he followed her into the bedroom she was more in command of herself. She stood in front of the dressing-table and began unfastening the ear-rings. Alex closed the bedroom door with slow deliberation and leaned against it.

'Now . . .' He drew in a deep breath and expelled it slowly. 'Now we'll talk.'

CHAPTER TWELVE

KATE ignored him. With her mouth set in grim silence she concentrated on removing the pearl jewellery as fast as she could. She replaced it all in the velvet box and snapped the lid shut.

'I have not lied to you, Kate. Not once.'

'You'd better put your jewellery away in a safe place,' she threw at him contemptuously as she headed for her dressing-room.

'It's yours. I bought it for you,' he insisted angrily.

She paused in the doorway, her eyes flashing scorn. 'Like hell you did! If you thought it would buy my complacence then you badly misjudged me.'

'I don't want your complacence. I . . .'

She shut the dressing-room door on his words and began stripping off the white dress. The door crashed open.

'God damn you Kate! I said we'd talk and we're going to talk!' Alex thundered at her.

She swung on him in a fury. 'Don't you tell me what I'm going to do. I'm not your possession. Our contract is broken. Now get out of my dressing-room and leave me alone!'

His face tightened up and he spoke with more control. 'You have no grounds for breaking our contract.'

'I didn't break it. You did.' She stepped out of the white dress and flung it at him. 'And here's your mockery of a bridal gown! Give it to Nicole Fouvet!'

The dress clung to him for a moment, then slithered to the floor. Kate met his eyes in fierce challenge but the torment she saw there wrenched at her heart. She turned away, opened a cupboard and snatched out a housecoat.

'You're my wife. I want no other.'

'You wanted her as your wife. The only hitch was that she wouldn't give you children,' Kate stated with cold precision as she viciously tightened the tie-belt of the cotton gown. 'She gave me chapter and verse, Alex, so don't bother lying to me.'

'Didn't it occur to you that Nicole might be lying?' he demanded harshly.

Kate faced him, her chin lifted in defiant accusation. 'She wasn't lying. The only reason you married me was to have children. I accepted that, Alex. I could have lived with that provided you kept to the terms of our contract. But you didn't tell me you loved another woman. I had to work that out for myself. And even that I could have lived with, provided you kept your promises. Tonight was the first test of how much your word was worth, and when I needed that faithful support you promised me, where were you, Alex?' She drew in a sharp breath and spat the words at him. 'You were with the woman you love.'

He had paled under the ferocity of her attack but not once had he dropped his gaze from hers. He looked at her now with pained eyes. 'I don't love Nicole Fouvet. I never did.'

Kate's mouth curled in derision. 'I'm not a

fool, Alex. I may not be as clever as you, certainly not as devious, but I'm not a fool. You love her. You revealed that to me the day we came home from our honeymoon. After your mother's visit your mind was full of Nicole, and my years with Scott taught me to recognise the times when he was thinking of someone else as he made love to me. You even apologised to me afterwards for . . . using me like that.' She sighed wearily and drove home the point. 'Did you think I didn't understand what was behind the apology?'

He bent his head and dragged a hand down his face as if wanting to wipe away the memory she had slapped there. 'I'm sorry,' he muttered, shaking his head as he turned away. 'I'm most terribly sorry that you felt that.' He leaned against the door-jamb and raked his fingers through his hair. 'How to make you understand? Where to even begin?'

'The picture is clear enough, Alex. Please stand aside and let me pass. I'll use a guest-room tonight.'

'No!'

Before she could evade his grasp he had swung back and caught hold of her arms, his fingers kneading the soft flesh while his eyes pleaded with her.

'You've got to listen to me, Kate. You've got it wrong. Wrong!' he repeated vehemently.

'You're hurting me, Alex.'

'Oh God!' He rubbed agitatedly at the places where his bruising fingers had dug in. 'I never wanted to hurt you, never meant to. Will you believe that much of me?'

She cast her mind back over their relationship

and conceded him that much. 'Yes, I don't think you meant me any harm, but you should have known I'd learn the truth sooner or later.'

'I was determined to keep to our contract, Kate. That's the truth. And I have, dammit!' he added more assertively. 'Tonight . . . just let me explain tonight. Come and sit down. Lie down. I won't touch you. You look exhausted.'

She was exhausted, fighting him now on brittle nerves which were ready to snap. She let him lead her over to the bed and waited tensely while he pulled back the bedclothes and piled all the pillows together to form a back-rest. Kate subsided against them and watched him walk away from her, wary of any movement to take advantage of her weak position.

'I'll start with Nicole,' he said abruptly, but stood for some time rubbing the back of his neck. Then he took off his jacket and tossed it carelessly towards a chair. His expression was morose when he turned to face her.

'My mother introduced her to me about six months ago. You saw how beautiful she is. I was completely infatuated . . . besotted.' He made a gesture of disgust and began pacing around. 'She seemed perfect to me. I was only too eager to give her whatever she asked, go anywhere, do anything. I thought I loved her but I was simply blinded by her beauty. It wasn't until she redecorated this house that I really began to see her clearly. By that time we were talking marriage, only her plans for the future didn't match mine.

'I began to feel uneasy but usually our arguments were left unresolved. We'd end up in bed and I'd think that was all I wanted. Then one night I brought up the subject of children. Nicole was surprised at my wanting to start a family at my age. She tried to laugh me out of it, but when it came right down to it, Nicole showed very clearly that not only did she not want children, she had no intention of giving me any. When I added it all up I looked at her and saw my mother . . . and I remembered my father.'

He gave a heavy sigh and sat down at the end of the bed. His shoulders hunched forward as he dropped his head in his hands. 'I remembered the fights when I was a kid . . . the long silences . . . Dad's heavy drinking . . . the day when I came home from school and my mother was gone . . . no goodbye . . . just gone . . .' He shuddered and straightened up. 'I finished with Nicole there and then, and I met you a week later.'

He stood and walked over to the dressing-table. He clicked open the velvet box and picked up the pearl necklace, fingering it as if appreciating its value. 'I met Mary Kathleen, who wanted nothing from me, who scorned the easy life I could offer her. She didn't want diamonds and pearls or fancy clothes. She had no ambition to shine in society. All she wanted was to have her children and a decent, family life. The complete contrast to Nicole.'

He dropped the jewellery into the box and turned to face her, his expresssion holding the same stern resolve which rang in his voice. 'I married you because I chose to share your future, not Nicole's. I didn't love you, Kate, but I wanted the kind of marriage you represented, and I was determined to make it work.'

His eyes softened. 'The strange thing was that your personal resistance to me was the challenge I needed to get my mind off Nicole. I set about remoulding your thoughts and reactions, and it was fascinating and rewarding to see you change. You slowly came out of your shell and started responding to me. I began to resent it when some part of you escaped me, when you hid your thoughts and pulled back from me. I wanted to know you completely.'

'But you kept so much of yourself back from me, Alex,' Kate said tiredly. He wasn't really telling her anything new, only filling in what she had already guessed. 'What about your reaction when Sonia Benelle . . .'

'Brought up Nicole's name? That made me take a good, hard look at our relationship, because it suddenly hit me that Nicole did not matter a damn any more. You were far more important to me than she had ever been.'

She made an impatient sound and closed her eyes. 'Now you're lying.'

Her eyes flew open in alarm as his weight depressed the mattress beside her. He took her hands in his, pressing them with urgent pursuasion. 'Kate, believe me. It's the truth.'

'It can't be,' she protested angrily. 'When your mother came . . .'

'While she was raving on about Nicole, I was thinking back over that sick obsession with her and I was disgusted that I had let myself be so . . . dominated by it. I looked at you and exulted over how lucky I was to have you as my wife.'

His hands released hers and lifted to gently cup her face. 'You, Mary Kathleen. And I wanted all of you so much . . .' His voice dropped to a husky whisper and the hungry longing in his eyes held her mesmerised, breathless. 'When my mother left I took you in my arms but you had that reserve in your eyes again, fending me off. I wanted to reach out, break through it, possess all of you. I felt . . . if only I could . . . Kate . . .'

The desperate plea was carried to her mouth as his kiss began seducing her resistance, sweeping her down a dizzying well of desire, demanding the answer to his own passion. Kate's need for his love brought a feverish response but the cancer of despair still gnawed at her heart. When his hand slid under her housecoat and closed over her breast, a chill of revulsion ripped through her. She pushed at him with all her strength.

'No! You're lying! Let me go! This is just what Scott used to do.'

His head jerked up. 'I am not Scott!' he grated out with savage emphasis. 'Will you forget that bastard once and for all?'

'How?' she cried, as savage in her protest as he. 'You're a carbon copy! You're counting on your lovemaking to gloss over . . .'

'No!' His fist crashed into the pillow beside her as his face worked convulsively to contain his frustration. 'I wasn't trying to . . .' He shook his head and dragged himself away from her, almost lurching across the room to the doors leading on to the balcony. He flung them open and stood there, his chest heaving as he drew in gulps of fresh air. Then in a voice charged with emotion, he asked, 'What do I have to do to reach you, Kate . . .? Or is it impossible?'

Her head was pounding with a turmoil of

thoughts. Her heart ached for him, but the one image which kept searing across her mind was the silhouette on the terrace. 'I can't ... I can't go through it again,' she muttered and pulled herself out of bed. She straightened her housecoat and began walking towards the door to the hallway.

'Don't go.'

He had turned. One shoulder was propped against the door-jamb. His hands were thrust into his pockets and his face looked haggard with failure. She hesitated, torn by her desire to go to him and her bitter resolve to be free of him.

'You can't walk out on our marriage on the basis of what you saw tonight. I wasn't unfaithful to you in thought or deed ... and you had my full support ... all the time.'

The dull weariness of his speech stabbed at her heart with far more force than his former vehemence.

'That's not true,' she choked out, tears glittering in her eyes.

'Isn't it, Kate? Let me tell you something. I've been happier in the last few days than I've ever been in my life. I didn't want to risk that happiness tonight. I knew my mother would have Nicole there and I knew the jolt to Nicole's ego would demand some retribution.

'But ...' he sighed, his shoulders lifting and slumping in a defeated shrug, '... I also knew we'd run into her sooner or later and I thought it was best to get it over with.'

A sardonic smile touched his lips. 'I wanted you dressed up, not for my pride, Kate, you had that wrong. It was to ensure that Nicole couldn't use her beauty as a line of attack. She tried ...'

The slight smile curled into a sneer of contempt. 'That proud promenade to greet us was planned to throw you off-balance. I was delighted when it didn't. Then when she made her play at me I was about to squash her arrogance with a public snub, but you suddenly jumped in and threw me off-balance with your show of indifference.

'That indifference knotted my stomach. I watched you all night, wondering what in hell was going on behind all the charming pleasantries. Then you slipped off to the powder room and my mother . . .' He sucked in a deep breath and his next words were bitten off with sharp sarcasm. 'My mother told me you were feeling a bit off-colour and I might find you out on the terrace. Needless to say it was Nicole who stepped out of the shrubbery.'

'And you stayed with her,' Kate put in bitterly.

His chin lifted and his eyes did not waver as he answered her charge. 'Yes, I stayed. I turned to leave and she called after me that she'd been speaking to you, that you'd said you didn't care if she and I were lovers, that all you wanted was for you and the children you had to be taken care of in the comfort I could provide.'

The blood drained from Kate's face as she realised how cleverly Nicole had twisted her words. 'Did you . . . did you believe her?' she dragged out painfully.

'You believed her,' he retorted with soft derision.

'Yes.' The word sounded hollow, echoing down all the empty places which that ravening cancer of despair had left behind.

'Well, I couldn't.' He shook his head. 'I

couldn't believe that you'd consent to infidelity. That was the first and most emphatic condition you laid down in our contract, and despite your show of indifference, I couldn't believe you were quite so indifferent to me either. In any case, I wasn't the least bit tempted by the idea of becoming Nicole's lover again, and I proceeded to tell her so in very precise terms. She threw her arms around me and tried to use the physical persuasion that used to work on me. I held her down and was telling her a few home-truths when you suddenly appeared.

'One look at your face told me I'd been judged and condemned. I stayed with Nicole just long enough to warn her that if she ever attempted to damage our marriage again I'd use whatever influence I could wield to get her blacklisted from society.'

He pushed himself away from the doorway and walked over to Kate with slow, deliberate steps. Kate stood still, completely drained of emotion. She could see it all so clearly now. Her own neurotic mistrust had conjured up her fears and fed the doubts and suspicions which grew all too easily, their seeds rooted in the corrupt soil of her marriage to Scott. She hung her head in shame, unable to look Alex in the eye when she had misjudged him so terribly. He gently laid his hands on her shoulders and she sagged under the weight of her guilt.

'Whatever you feel about me, Kate, you signed a contract and it stands. You're already carrying my child and I won't let you go.'

She swallowed hard in an effort to moisten her dry throat. She had to speak, tell him she did not want to go, that all she wanted was to be with him. Before the right words could be formed a strident ringing echoed through the house. Harsh, repeated jabs of the doorbell demanded attention. Alex's hands squeezed her shoulders and he sighed, a long, shuddering breath.

'Stay here. I'll answer it.'

His voice was flat. She watched him walk away from her, his shoulders slumped with the fatigue of having fought a fight and reached stalemate. Her heart cried out for him but still she could not find voice. He closed the door after him and Kate felt a sharp echo of the desolation she had suffered earlier.

You fool! You fool! Go after him. Tell him how you feel, her mind screamed. At last her body obeyed, stiffly at first, reluctant even now to give that final, irrevocable surrender. Her heart was pounding, fear and need beating their conflicting drums. She reached for the door, opened it.

Alex's voice floated back to her. 'It's all right, Mrs Beatty. I'll get it. Go back to bed.'

Kate hesitated, not wanting to face the housekeeper. She suddenly realised there would be a visitor to face too and her willpower teetered as all the long-held inhibitions fought against her decision. Alex had told her to wait. But who was the visitor calling at this hour? Nicole? Surely not if Alex had told the truth. And she believed him, didn't she? Then who?

Forcing one foot in front of another she walked to where the balustrade began its sweeping curve. Still protected from view by the wall of the hallway she peered down to the foyer where Alex was just opening the front door.

CHAPTER THIRTEEN

VERA PALLISTER swept past him in a flurry of chiffon. Kate jerked back into hiding. She could not face Alex's mother. Alex would send her away. Surely he would send her away. He could no more want his mother here than Kate did. Vera had put them both through too much agony of mind tonight. Kate leaned back against the wall and closed her eyes, waiting to hear the inevitable dismissal before going down to Alex.

'What are you doing here?' His voice was weary beyond measure. 'The game is over. You played it very well, Mother. Too well. Go home. Just go home and leave us alone. Rest on your laurels. You won.'

'No. You don't understand . . .'

The words were quick, urgent, interrupted by a crashing thump, then Alex's voice in harsh accusation.

'God damn you! You couldn't just sit this one out, could you? You had to pick the one gambit, the one dirty play which . . .'

'Why did you provoke me into it?' Vera retorted fiercely. 'All you had to do was tell me.'

'When did you or I ever tell each other anything?'

'You would never listen.'

'Oh, I listened, Mother. I listened to the silence thirty years ago. It was more eloquent than words.'

'You've paid me back for that mistake a thousand times, and now you've led me into hurting that poor girl. You could have told me this time. Been straight with me for once. Weren't her feelings important enough for you to put aside your revenge on me?'

It was a passionate defence and Alex's voice held a note of incredulity when he replied.

'My revenge?'

'What do you call your silence, your refusal to share anything with me? It was your game, Alex. You started it. All these years I've played it your way because it was the only way to have you in my life. But it's been a sick, sadistic, catch-me-if-you-can game, and God forgive me, I came to enjoy the little triumphs I had. But it was no triumph for me tonight to see the pain and despair on your wife's face. Why, in God's name, did you stay out there with Nicole? It was cruel, Alex.'

'You can say that to me! You set up the whole bloody scene.'

'Yes, and for that I have to bear the guilt but you ... you must have known Kate loved you. How could you play with her so ... so wickedly, just to spite me.'

'No!'

Kate was riveted to the spot, her heart thudding in her ears and her fingernails digging into her palms as she waited for Alex's reaction to Vera's words. The harshly indrawn breath was clearly audible.

'I thought I could control it.' The words were forced out, strained with intense regret. 'But you're wrong, Mother. I didn't stay with Nicole out of any desire for her, and Kate ... Kate doesn't love me.'

'Stop fencing with me, Alex. You said the game was over. Hurting each other is one thing. We're old hands at it. But that girl loves you. Do you think I'm blind?'

'No ... not blind. I've no doubt you saw her pain but you mistook the cause.'

The weary defeat was back in his voice. It curled around Kate's heart and she pushed herself away from the wall, determined to go to him. But Vera was speaking again, a torrent of pain from all their years of estrangement.

'Then tell me. Let me understand. For once in your life give me credit for some humanity. I know you hold me in contempt. But I also know what it's like to feel love and pain and despair. And you ... you're so proud and ruthless, Alex. I came because I'm ashamed of both of us, ashamed of what we did tonight. If there's anything I can do to fix the situation I'll do it.'

'There's nothing ... nothing you can do. The pain is rooted in the past. Kate's first husband was a slick philanderer. He even had his current mistress on my yacht the day he died. Kate didn't love me, or even want me. I persuaded her into marriage with the promise of children and security.

'She was like a broken doll, trying to walk on her own, wounded, but so proud, so fiercely independent. I took her as my wife and I began mending her, putting back the stuffing, sewing up the tears and smoothing over the cracks. I think she was almost whole again ... until tonight. She thought ... she thought I was being unfaithful to her, like Scott, and now she's right back where we started, not trusting anybody.

'I just can't get through to her. As for me, Nicole means less than nothing, Kate is everything. So there's your answer, Mother. Is that what you wanted to know?'

Kate was impelled to interrupt now. She could not let Alex go on suffering so needlessly. She took a step forward and glanced down. He was sitting dejectedly on one of the bottom stairs. Vera leaned forward and touched his shoulder.

'If I talked to Kate . . . explained . . .'

He shook his head. 'It wouldn't help. I've just got to start again, building up her confidence in me.'

'Could . . . could we start again, Alex?'

There was so much wretched hope in Vera's voice that Kate hesitated, loath to break into what might become a reconciliation.

'It's a bit late for us, isn't it, Mother?' Alex replied sardonically.

'You said the game was over. Do we have to go on fighting?'

'No.' He nodded a couple of times. 'You're right. Let's end it if we can. Kate has no one, Mother. Her family's in Tasmania and Scott's friends . . . she called them rats and that was exactly what they were. Do you think you could . . . no, she'd think . . .'

'I can try, can't I? I'd like to try.'

'It's not going to be easy after tonight.'

'I know.'

'She keeps a hard, protective shell around her.'

'So I observed. It had me fooled until I saw . . .

Alex, are you sure she doesn't love you? I could've sworn . . .'

Kate's cheeks scorched with the heat of embarrassment. Her eavesdropping was fast becoming too painful to admit. Alex shook his head.

'No. Sometimes I've felt . . . No, I don't know what Kate feels. She doesn't trust me. She gives me so much and then retreats. I must go back to her.'

'Yes, of course. I'm sorry if my coming interrupted . . .'

'No.' Alex stood up and stretched his back tiredly. 'She probably needed time away from me to think. Maybe we can talk more rationally when I go back upstairs. It was . . . good of you to come.'

He moved to the door and Vera followed. She touched his arm and he looked at her.

'Alex, it wasn't that I didn't love you. I was hitting back at your father . . . And then you hated me.'

'We'll talk about it,' he said with a wry gentleness.

'You'll listen?' Vera's voice was tremulous.

'Yes. I think it's time I listened.'

'Alex, let me give you some good advice. Tell Kate that you love her. Your father and I . . . we stopped telling each other . . . Tell her, and keep telling her until she believes it.'

'I can't. She doesn't want that from me. Not yet.'

'Yes I do.'

Kate's voice rang out firmly, very positive in its statement. They looked up at her, two faces in startled concern. Kate moved with determination, a self-conscious dignity carrying her down the stairs as she continued speaking.

'I couldn't stay in the bedroom, Alex. I'm sorry, but I couldn't bear your walking away from me when I hadn't even responded to you. I've been afraid of so many things, afraid of loving you and afraid of losing you, especially tonight. It was wrong of me to listen but I couldn't face your mother, and when you began speaking, I couldn't walk away from what you were saying. I can see now that I've hidden from you for too long. Your mother's right. I do love you, and I desperately need your assurance that you love me.'

There was stunned disbelief on his face, a quiet smile of relief on Vera's. With courage riding high, Kate stepped on to the marble floor of the foyer and moved straight to Alex's mother.

'Thank you for coming, Vera. Perhaps you'd like to have dinner with us tomorrow night.'

'I'd like that very much. Please call me tomorrow. Good night, my dear.'

She made a swift exit. Kate turned to Alex, her eyes pleading for understanding and forgiveness. He stepped closer, a conflict of emotions struggling for supremacy. One hand lifted and touched her cheek wonderingly.

'You love me, Kate?'

A light flush stole over her cheeks and her voice trembled as she delivered her total surrender. 'I really couldn't help it, Alex. You just took over my heart, bit by bit, until you owned it completely.'

'I own it?'

Still there was a question.

'You do.' She smiled and all her love for him flowed out in an exultant stream, bathing him in unmistakable warmth.

'Oh God! I thought you'd never surrender.' He gathered her to him in a fiercely possessive embrace. For a long, poignant moment he simply held her. Then in a voice choked with emotion he whispered, 'I love you so very much, Mary Kathleen.'

Her full name sounded wonderful, very special and uniquely blessed, a warm caress of love.

'I'll treasure your love all my life,' he continued huskily. 'You'll never have cause to doubt what I feel for you. You're everything I ever yearned for and more.'

She sighed with utter contentment. 'I'll never doubt you again, Alex. I promise.'

'No more of Scott.' He tilted her head back, searching her eyes with urgent intensity. 'Has he gone, Kate? Are you really mine?'

'As I learned to love you I realised that I'd never really loved Scott,' she answered with devastating simplicity.

The deep joy she felt was suddenly reflected in his eyes. He kissed her and it was a promise of such complete fulfilment that elation whipped through her veins as he swept her up into his arms and strode upstairs. She clung to him, pressing kisses to his throat, nibbling his ear, pouring out a chant of love.

It was a long, long time before another coherent word was spoken. They lay entwined, their bodies languourous in the aftermath of the most beautiful lovemaking of all, the gift of each other in total commitment.

'When did you know?' Alex asked softly, uncaring now of the torment that was safely past.

'Oh, I kept fighting you off all the time, but I had to finally admit it to myself that afternoon when we came home.'

He sighed and ran a caressing hand over her lightly rounded stomach. 'I wish I'd spoken then. I almost did when you told me about the baby. It was all I could do not to show you how much you meant to me.'

'I felt it. I thought it was for the child.'

'That too, but I was bursting with love for you. We were such fools, hiding what we felt from each other.'

'Well, it was supposed to be a marriage of convenience,' she reminded him teasingly.

He grinned. 'Oh, I don't know. I was instinctively drawn to you right from the beginning, Mary Kathleen.'

'Well . . . if the truth be told, you had a pretty strong effect on me too. I just didn't want to get emotionally involved with anyone.' She sighed happily and snuggled closer. 'We're terribly lucky, aren't we?'

'Lucky? Nonsense! We've both got good judgment.'

She laughed up at him. 'Are you wearing a smug smile, Alex Dalton?'

'If I am, it's because I'm gloatingly, gloriously happy, and I've got my love to keep me warm.'

She smiled smugly. 'Me too.'

Here's how to get this special offer from Harlequin! As simple as 1…2…3!

OCTOBER
TREASURY EDITION
COUPON

1. Each month, save one Treasury Edition coupon from your favorite Romance or Presents novel.
2. In four months you'll have saved four Treasury Edition coupons (only one coupon per month allowed).
3. Then all you have to do is fill out and return the order form provided, along with the four Treasury Edition coupons required and $1.00 for postage and handling.

Mail to: Harlequin Reader Service

In the U.S.A.
2504 West Southern Ave.
Tempe, AZ 85282

In Canada
P.O. Box 2800, Postal Station A
5170 Yonge Street
Willowdale, Ont. M2N 6J3

RT1-C-2

Please send me my FREE copy of the Janet Dailey Treasury Edition. I have enclosed the four Treasury Edition coupons required and $1.00 for postage and handling along with this order form.

(Please Print)

NAME_____

ADDRESS_____

CITY_____

STATE/PROV._____ ZIP/POSTAL CODE_____

SIGNATURE_____

This offer is limited to one order per household.

SUPPLIES LIMITED

This special Janet Dailey offer expires January 1986.

·H·A·R·L·E·Q·U·I·N·

FIRST·CLASS

Sweepstakes

OFFICIAL RULES

1. **NO PURCHASE NECESSARY.** To enter, complete the official entry/order form. Be sure to indicate whether or not you wish to take advantage of our subscription offer.

2. Entry blanks have been preselected for the prizes offered. Your response will be checked to see if you are a winner. In the event that these preselected responses are not claimed, a random drawing will be held from all entries received to award not less than $150,000 in prizes. This is in addition to any free, surprise or mystery gifts which might be offered. Versions of this sweepstakes with different prizes will appear in Preview Service Mailings by Harlequin Books and their affiliates. Winners selected will receive the prize offered in their sweepstakes brochure.

3. This promotion is being conducted under the supervision of Marden-Kane, an independent judging organization. By entering the sweepstakes, each entrant accepts and agrees to be bound by these rules and the decisions of the judges, which shall be final and binding. Odds of winning in the random drawing are dependent upon the total number of entries received. Taxes, if any, are the sole responsibility of the prize winners. Prizes are nontransferable. All entries must be received by August 31, 1986.

4. The following prizes will be awarded:

   (1) Grand Prize: Rolls-Royce™ or $100,000 Cash!
   (Rolls-Royce being offered by permission of Rolls-Royce Motors Inc.)

   (1) Second Prize: A trip for two to Paris for 7 days/6 nights. Trip includes air transportation on the Concorde, hotel accommodations...PLUS...$5,000 spending money!

   (1) Third Prize: A luxurious Mink Coat!

5. This offer is open to residents of the U.S. and Canada, 18 years or older, except employees of Harlequin Books, its affiliates, subsidiaries, Marden-Kane and all other agencies and persons connected with conducting this sweepstakes. All Federal, State and local laws apply. Void in the province of Quebec and wherever prohibited or restricted by law. Winners will be notified by mail and may be required to execute an affidavit of eligibility and release, which must be returned within 14 days after notification. Canadian winners will be required to answer a skill-testing question. Winners consent to the use of their name, photograph and/or likeness for advertising and publicity purposes in conjunction with this and similar promotions without additional compensation. One prize per family or household.

6. For a list of our most current prize winners, send a stamped, self-addressed envelope to: WINNERS LIST, c/o Marden-Kane, P.O. Box 10404, Long Island City, New York 11101

You're invited to accept 4 books and a surprise gift Free!

Acceptance Card

Mail to: **Harlequin Reader Service®**

In the U.S.
2504 West Southern Ave.
Tempe, AZ 85282

In Canada
P.O. Box 2800, Postal Station A
5170 Yonge Street
Willowdale, Ontario M2N 6J3

YES! Please send me 4 free Harlequin Presents® novels and my free surprise gift. Then send me 8 brand new novels every month as they come off the presses. Bill me at the low price of $1.75 each ($1.95 in Canada)—an 11% saving off the retail price. There are no shipping, handling or other hidden costs. There is no minimum number of books I must purchase. I can always return a shipment and cancel at any time. Even if I never buy another book from Harlequin, the 4 free novels and the surprise gift are mine to keep forever.   108 BPP-BPGE

Name _____ (PLEASE PRINT)

Address _____ Apt. No. _____

City _____ State/Prov. _____ Zip/Postal Code _____

This offer is limited to one order per household and not valid to present subscribers. Price is subject to change.   ACP-SUB-1